CURSE OF LIES AND SHADOW

CURSE OF LIES AND SHADOW

THE SHADOW MARKED: BOOK ONE

JESSICA LEMORE

For everyone searching for love.

CONTENTS

POPPY

*N*o matter how hard I try, I can't shake the feeling that someone's watching me. They're in the warm breeze as it wraps around my body, lifting the hair off my neck. They're in the stir of the leaves, a symphony on repeat. When I'm alone, they're the shadow creeping forward, marking me.

"Poppy Mathews," a voice called.

The room fell silent, the change so sharp it broke my concentration from the notebook. I looked up to find every eye on me. A few quiet chuckles rang out across the large lecture hall. My eyes met Professor Brumley's steel-gray gaze and my stomach dropped. Everyone was waiting for my answer to a question I hadn't even heard.

Yet again, words failed me—figuratively and literally. My hastily written musings distracted me from the lecture, and I couldn't make sense of the jumbled thoughts swirling in my head to ask him to repeat the question.

Professor B shook his head slightly before moving on, his eyes darting around those in the room. "You're paying good money to be here. The least you could do is pay attention."

My gaze drifted back to my notebook. The center of attention wasn't what I strived for. Usually, I had the uncanny ability to disappear in a crowd. There was nothing about me that stood out. I was ordinary, easily average, and that's why I had been caught so off guard.

At the front of the lecture hall, Mr. B stopped pacing. "Would anyone like to answer? Is Shylock a victim? A villain? Something in between?"

I sank deeper into my seat. A few hands shot up into the air. I breathed a sigh of relief when he called on a boy near the front. I turned the page of the notebook, pen poised to take notes. My second-to-last semester at White Bridge University was almost over. I could save the distractions for winter break.

That is, if I passed Mr. B's class.

I hadn't even wanted to take Shakespeare, but my adviser recommended it. I needed an elective. I couldn't settle on anything that sounded interesting. So here I was, struggling through iambic pentameter.

"Poppy," the whisper met my ears.

The hair on my neck prickled, and I dropped my pen. I slowly turned but saw nothing out of the ordinary. Everyone was scribbling in their notebooks, actually paying attention. No one had called my name.

The boy behind me looked up, his dark brown eyes meeting mine. He cocked an eyebrow. I could only assume he wanted to know why I was looking at him. I turned back in my seat, sliding down to further hide myself.

"Papers are due Monday," Mr. B said, drawing me back to reality.

I closed my notebook and threw it in my bag. Now that the last class of the week was over, I could finally go home. I was exhausted—as evidenced by the fact that I was hearing my name when no one had been calling it.

My phone vibrated when I stood. I quickly glanced at it.

We're going to McLaughlin's. I'll pick you up at 8.

I didn't respond to the text. What was the point? Even if I said no, Addie would still show up at 8. That's what best friends do. They don't let you wallow in your depression. As I made my way through the quad, I picked up my pace. I couldn't risk seeing George.

Four days ago, George Vanderwalt broke up with me. I hadn't been expecting it. How could I? He had just told me he loved me. We were making plans for summer break. I was supposed to go to his house for dinner tomorrow night. My stomach sank as his words echoed in my head: *"I don't think I really love you. It just . . . doesn't feel like it's supposed to."* What did that even mean? What's love supposed to feel like?

We had been dating for four years. We had met in high school. We were going to leave White Bridge together. I even thought we would get married.

When I reached my car, I let out the breath I had been holding. While I had been grateful I hadn't seen George, a small part of me hoped I would. Maybe if he saw me again, he would change his mind. Maybe he missed me.

I inserted the key in the ignition and jumped when loud music filled the silence. I quickly reached for the volume, turning it off. My morning and evening self were two different beings—one highly caffeinated and overly anxious, thinking the loud music would calm my nerves; the other quiet and reflective of the day.

The drive home was uneventful, which gave me ample time to replay my embarrassment in Shakespeare. It was hard enough to make friends at school. I didn't live on campus or have an apartment. I still lived at home with my parents. I was only on campus for class. There were no clubs, sororities, or sports I was interested in joining, but at least I had Addie Whitlock.

We had been friends since our senior year of high school, and while we attended the same college, she was making her way through the pre-med track, so we had no classes together.

When I pulled into the driveway, I noticed it was empty. My parents' car was gone. I glanced at the dashboard: 6:30. They were usually home by now. I looked at my phone—no missed calls, no text messages.

Everything was silent when I stepped out of the car. The crisp November air clung to me, and I shivered. We were lucky we hadn't had any snow. It could be beautiful, peaceful even, but I hated it. I hated how cold it got. I hated how it covered everything, blanketing the once vibrant green grass in piles of dirty slush.

When I was inside, I tossed my bag on the kitchen table before making my way to the light switch across the room. For the second time that day, the hair on the back of my neck prickled. I flipped the light switch and turned around. In the shadows of the dining room, I could just make out the outline of a person.

On instinct, I stepped closer, trying to see through the darkness.

"Mom? Dad?"

Outside, a car turned down the road, the headlights illuminating the room for only a moment. A tall man looked back at me. His broad shoulders slackened, and his black jacket opened at the neck, revealing large tattoos. I stepped backward, a scream escaping my lips. The headlights vanished, shrouding the room in darkness again.

Before I could move, another car turned down the road, illuminating the dining room once more.

It was empty.

POPPY

Mwy heart hammered so loudly I couldn't think straight. Had I really seen someone? Had it been a trick of the light? A shadow?

Silence surrounded me as I contemplated my options. I could keep standing in the kitchen or I could leave.

When my brain finally kicked in, I ran for the door.

I stepped outside, and headlights greeted me. A car slowly pulled into the driveway. I strained my eyes, exhaling the breath I had been holding when I recognized my parents. I ran to the driveway, waving my hands in the air to get their attention. The car stopped and the driver's door opened.

"Pop?" my father's uneasy voice came. "What's wrong? Are you okay?"

I ran to him. How was I supposed to answer? Should I tell him I thought I saw someone in the house? What if it had only been a trick of the light? "I was in the kitchen; a car drove by and their headlights..." I moved behind the driver's side door, trying to put as much distance as I could between me and the house. "A man was in the dining room . . . but maybe it was only my imagination. Maybe it was the darkness playing tricks on me."

He pushed me into the driver's seat. "Let me check. Emilia, you have your phone?"

My mother nodded, rummaging in her purse for her cell. I closed the door. Warm air blasted my face when I leaned over the steering wheel. Outside, my father reached inside his jacket to withdraw a silver pocketknife.

I turned to my mom. "Where did that come from?"

I had never seen my father with anything sharper than a butter knife. My gaze fell back to the windshield as he stalked through the shadows, knife poised.

"He always carries that," she answered. "Lock the doors."

I pressed the lock button, the click echoing around us. I reached for my phone but realized I had left it inside. A hand fell on my arm, and I turned to find my mother, her warm gaze settling on me.

"Everything will be all right. No matter what happens."

My eyes narrowed, trying to make sense of her statement. What an odd thing to say. I was going to ask her what that meant when the house pulled my attention again. Lights turned on—first the kitchen, followed by the dining room, then the living room, before moving upstairs.

I held my breath, waiting for something to happen. Was the man still inside? If so, what did he want? A chill snaked down my spine. Maybe I had imagined him like I had imagined someone saying my name in class. Was the stress of my first breakup, coupled with the hard semester of college, finally getting to me?

When my father reappeared, he was no longer holding the knife. My mother removed her hand from my arm. She smiled softly, the corners of her mouth crinkling. She opened the door and joined my father. From the driver's seat, I watched their exchange, glad I couldn't hear them. They were probably discussing the best way to deal with my hallucination.

When they both looked up, meeting my gaze, I opened the door slowly.

"Maybe we should call the cops?" I asked.

"No need," my father called. "There's no one inside. I think I know what startled you."

I swallowed, waiting for him to continue, to explain what I had seen. Maybe there was a rational explanation. Maybe I wasn't losing my mind.

"Come inside," he added, turning back to the house. "I'll make some tea."

I stepped forward. "What about the car?"

"I got it," my mother said. "My purse is still in there."

A cool breeze blew past me, lifting the hair off my neck slightly. The crescent moon smiled down on me, serenely watching my breakdown. Another car passed our house as I followed my steps from earlier. My muscles tensed as I climbed the stairs to the back porch.

"Here, Pop," my father called, "I'll show you."

As I crossed the threshold, he moved to the entrance of the dining room, opposite the backdoor. He leaned against the frame, pointing to the jacket hanging off the back of a chair. My mom hated when he left his jackets at the dining room table. *"Chairs aren't coat racks."*

"I was in a hurry this morning," he said. "That must be what you saw."

My mind raced. He didn't think I mistook a jacket for a person, did he? I shook my head. "That wasn't what I saw."

He sighed. "Either way, no one's in the house. Nothing's taken. It must have been a trick of the light."

The door flew open, startling me from the conversation. My hand flew to my chest as my mother walked in, dropping her purse to the counter. My father crossed the kitchen, helping her out of her coat. He kissed her cheek before locking the backdoor.

Their minor acts of love never escaped me. From a distance, I watched their displays of affection with mild interest, knowing one day I would find my person, the one I would spend the rest of my life with. When I met George, I thought I had found it.

"Who wants tea?" my father asked.

"I would love a cup," my mother answered. "What are your plans tonight, Poppy? Going out with George?"

I turned away, hoping to hide from the question. I still hadn't told them about the breakup. How could I? My mom loved George. Secretly, I hoped I wouldn't have to tell her. A part of me figured we would be back together before the end of the week. "I'm going to McLaughlin's with Addie," I answered. "I won't be home too late. I'm tired."

She nodded, flipping through the mail they must have picked up before pulling into the driveway. I crossed my arms over my chest, listening for any noises to indicate someone else was in the house with us. When the teapot cried out, my father turned off the stovetop.

A dull ache pierced my forehead. What was wrong with me? My parents didn't seem concerned. There was obviously no one in the house with us.

"I guess I'm going to get ready," I said, breaking the silence that had fallen over us. "Addie will be here soon."

"Have fun, sweetie," my mom called, her eyes never leaving the mail.

My father looked as if he wanted to say something but couldn't form the words. I paused, giving him a moment. When he turned back to the tea, I slowly made my way out of the kitchen. Perhaps the breakup was affecting me more than I realized.

I had only made it to the stairs when my father's low voice carried, "Maybe she should stay home."

"She's fine," my mother answered. "The new moon already passed. It was only shadows."

My eyes flew to the window, searching the darkness. My mother had always been fixated on the moon. Her response didn't surprise me. Growing up, she planned our nights out around the phases of the moon. She was convinced the new moon was for staying at home, relaxing with family. To this day, I still don't understand, but humor her, nonetheless.

I strained my ears once more, listening for any signs of the man. All the pent-up tension dissolved when silence met me.

The cold air pulled at me as I ran down the front steps and crossed the driveway. That had been close. Poppy had actually seen me. I had told myself I wasn't going in this time, but the need to see her, to protect her, overtook everything else. I ran into the thick line of trees bordering the property, disappearing in shadow.

Across the street, headlights appeared. A car pulled up to the mailbox, the engine idling. Emilia and Flinn. My stomach churned, the anger rising as Poppy's parents came into view.

The people of this land had a saying that time heals all wounds. I chuckled. In my case, time seemed to make it worse. Even though I couldn't blame them for leaving Marwood after the decree, the resentment clung to me. Hadn't they realized the danger they'd put her in?

The backdoor to the house flew open. I slid further into darkness when Poppy appeared. She ran to her parents' car as they pulled into the driveway. I crouched, hiding behind the tall brush.

My phone vibrated. Only one other person knew this number. Cerros.

I withdrew the phone, swiping the screen to answer. "What."

My brother didn't even acknowledge my tone. My greeting hadn't been a question, but rather a statement. "No sign of them."

I leaned against the tree trunk next to me. "We can't be too careful."

The line crackled as if it was going to disconnect.

My eyes drifted to Poppy. She was now in her parents' car.

"How much longer are you going to do this?" he asked. "How much longer are you going to hide in shadow?"

I pressed my lips together; my jaw hard. Even though I found it ironic—hiding in shadow—I wasn't in the mood for his chiding. "She doesn't even remember me. What am I supposed to do?"

"Take her," he answered simply. "You're fated."

His tone infuriated me. He hadn't gone through the decree. He didn't understand the need to protect his fated, even against us—our family.

He cleared his throat. "Are you on your way back? I'm ready to go home."

"You're free to leave," I answered. "We're no longer bound by the moon."

Once I learned Poppy had been taken to this land, I sought the best potion-makers, those gifted in natural magic. We no longer needed the new moon to travel between worlds. My brother and I could come and go at our leisure. But so could our enemies.

When Cerros said nothing, my stomach clenched. He didn't have to help. He didn't have to be here. As the next in line to the throne, he had enough on his plate in Marwood.

"Thank you," I continued. "For coming with me. I can always count on you."

He exhaled loudly. "I'll always be here for you, Thaniel. Even if I don't understand."

Poppy moved from the car. Her long brown hair fell down her back. A part of me wanted to run to her, to scoop her in my arms and take her home. If she returned to Marwood, her memories would come back. She would remember me.

"She saw me," I said. "I had been inside, checking the house. I hadn't heard her come in."

"Did she recognize you?"

Poppy stopped walking as if she had heard my brother's question. The breeze curled around her as she looked at the moon. My heart hammered in my chest. I would give anything for her to remember.

"No," I finally said.

His tone softened as he continued, "Are you on your way back?"

"I'm going to keep watch on the house a little longer," I answered.

Poppy tore her gaze from the inky sky. She ran up the stairs to the back porch. What had her parents told her? They must know I found her. It couldn't have been a surprise. Would they run again?

"Next time you see her, maybe introduce yourself," he said.

I chuckled. "What would I even say? My name's Thaniel Ashton-Dumont. I'm your fated. After learning of our decree, your parents used magic to suppress your memories. They gave you a new identity in a new world."

"Don't forget to tell her you're a prince," he added cheekily. "Oh, and that our family is Shadow Marked."

A small shiver passed through me at the mention of our family's curse. My head lowered, my gaze falling on the large tattoos crawling up my chest to my neck. Even though my shirt and jacket covered most of them, they were still noticeable. "That'll only scare her away."

"Will it?" he asked. "She didn't have a problem with it before."

"I hadn't activated the curse."

Static muted his response. A car turned onto the road and loud, angry music filled my ears. My head clouded. I didn't understand the music of this land.

When the car passed, I could just make out my brother's voice. "I'll keep up my surveillance."

Instinctively, I nodded. I stopped when I realized he couldn't see me. "Thank you."

I disconnected the call. Even though Poppy was safely inside, I couldn't relax. My muscles tensed as I crouched lower, my eyes trained on the house. After pulling the car further into the driveway, Emilia slammed the door shut. Before heading inside, she paused, her eyes roaming the forest line. A moment later, she made her way inside.

I slid the phone into my pocket before searching the perimeter. When they fled Marwood, one thing Emilia and Flinn failed to take into consideration was that my family had enemies, and because Poppy was my fated, they were now her enemies.

But I would do anything to keep her safe.

POPPY

*A*ddie maneuvered the car off the highway. She jerked the steering wheel to the right, narrowly missing a pothole. I gripped the seat tighter, my fingers digging into the upholstery. Even though I was used to her driving, my nerves were already frayed, shattered by the events of the day.

"So," Addie began, "what did he look like?"

My stomach lurched as the car swerved again. "Can you slow down?"

"Do you want to get there?"

When she let up on the gas pedal, I peeled my eyes from the road. "Safely, yes."

"You know, there's a name for this kind of anxiety. I believe it's called amaxophobia. Look it up. It may be helpful to bring up at your next doctor's appointment."

I ignored her diagnosis. It couldn't possibly be induced by her careless driving. I loosened my hold on the seat, relaxing my fingers slightly. I closed my eyes, bringing forth the image of the man.

"He was tall," I began, answering Addie's original question. "At least six feet. Oh, and he had these tattoos on his chest that made their way up his neck." I opened my eyes. "It felt so real. The way he looked at me, it was almost like he was surprised to see me."

"Did he say anything?"

I shook my head. "No. When the headlights lit up the room again, it was empty. Did I hallucinate him? No one was in the house."

Addie parked the car. After removing the key from the ignition, she turned to me. "It could be stress," she said, her voice soft. "George did just break up with you. This semester has been hard."

I nodded, exhaling my pent-up breath. "Do you think we'll get back together?"

"You don't want George," she said. "You'll find someone who will move heaven and earth to be with you. Don't settle. If you see him tonight, remember all he put you through this week."

My vision blurred. I quickly reached up and wiped away the tears. Addie could be hard, reckless even, but she was the best friend I could have ever asked for.

She squeezed my arm before reaching over and pulling the visor down, revealing a mirror. "Fix your makeup. I don't want to be known as crying girl's friend. I'm hoping the hottie from last week's here."

I wiped the last tears from my face. Addie handed me her concealer, and I went to work fixing my makeup.

"He's here," she squealed a moment later.

I followed her gaze, spying her latest crush near the entrance. He was with a large group of people, all talking excitedly. The girl next to him began dancing, twirling on her tiptoes as they waited to be let in.

Addie threw her jacket in the backseat. "Hurry up. I want to talk to him."

I snapped the visor shut. She stepped outside, and I quickly removed my jacket, hoping she wouldn't leave without me. I opened my door and immediately regretted it when a frigid blast of air met me. I looked back at the entrance; thankful the line was moving quickly.

Addie ran her hands through her hair before turning her attention to her outfit. She adjusted the straps of her black-lace dress, pulling the fabric down to reveal more cleavage. The dress was beautiful, and it hugged every curve of her toned body.

A boy with sandy-brown hair walked by us, eyeing her hungrily and ignoring me completely. I shifted awkwardly on my feet, my eyes moving to my dark-blue dress. It didn't hug my body the same way hers did.

"Ready?" she asked, completely oblivious to the boy's stare.

I nodded. Through the window, I eyed my jacket, wishing I could at least wear it inside, but the bar didn't have a coat check. Addie pressed her key fob, locking the car as she made her way across the street. I followed when I remembered my cell phone. It was still in my jacket, tucked in the pocket.

"I left my phone in the car," I called out.

Addie didn't even stop. "You won't need it."

I looked back at the car one last time before following her across the street. By the time we got to the entrance, her crush had already gone inside. After we paid our entrance fee, I followed Addie into the dark bar, bypassing groups of excited people.

The music was so loud it echoed in my head, making me dizzy. When the familiar, stale, earthy scent hit me, I froze. The last time I had been here was with George.

Addie took my hand, wrapping her long fingers around mine. She led us to the middle of the dance floor. "Come on," she said, jumping to the beat, "shake the day off."

I followed her lead, losing myself for a moment. I closed my eyes, dancing out the stress from George, Shakespeare, and the *hallucinations.* For a moment, I wished I had brought my phone. Maybe George had called me. Maybe he was here.

Addie dropped my hand, and I opened my eyes. Her crush was whispering in her ear. Leave it to Addie. She always got what she wanted.

When she looked up, she winked—our signal that she was okay with the attention. What surprised me was that her crush was in my Shakespeare class. He sat behind me. He had caught me staring at him after I heard my name.

"I'll be right back!" I shouted, hoping she would hear me over the music.

When she leaned forward, her brow crinkled. I pointed to the bathroom. She nodded before turning around so she was facing him. She wrapped her arms around his neck.

I stepped into the pulsating crowd. What was I going to do now that Addie was preoccupied? I didn't want to be a third wheel. Usually, I had George to dance with. Now I was alone.

The bathrooms were in a long hallway near the back. I pushed through a group of girls, all looking at their phones, only to find George. My stomach sank. He was dancing with someone. His arms were wrapped around her waist. She was leaning into him, stroking his hair. An elbow hit me from behind, but I couldn't move. I was rooted to the scene before me.

George was completely oblivious to my presence. Somehow, he leaned even closer to his date, brushing his lips over hers. The room spun. My breath quickened as everything around me blurred.

The couple behind them moved toward the bar, revealing a tall man in a black jacket. His back was against the wall, his arms crossed over his chest. His blue eyes moved from George to me. When our eyes finally met, everything around me faded. It was as if we were the only two people in the room. He uncrossed his arms and pushed off the wall.

As if awakening from a bad dream, everything came into focus again. The room was packed, the music loud. I blinked, trying to clear my vision. The man continued to watch me as he stepped forward.

A pit formed in my stomach when I recognized him. He had been in my house earlier. Who was he? What did he want? My legs didn't seem to want to move.

The man pushed his way through George and his date, separating them from their kiss. George yelled, but the man continued forward, ignoring him. I stepped back, bumping into the person behind me. Before entering the crowd, I mumbled an apology. I had to find Addie.

The music echoed in my head, the frantic beat piercing me. I turned back. He was still following me. My mouth ran dry. I picked up my pace, willing my legs to move faster. My logical self couldn't make sense of what was happening. Why would a stranger be following me?

When I neared the dance floor, I searched for Addie but didn't see her. I turned, finding a large group of people near the long oak bar. I weaseled my way between them, hoping to lose the man in the crowd. Without stopping to look back, I circled toward the bathrooms. Somewhere along the way, someone spilled soda on me, but I didn't stop. Once I reached the bathroom, I could lock the door. Hopefully that's where Addie was.

I had almost reached the hallway when a pair of strong arms gripped me from behind, pulling me through the emergency exit. I found myself outside. The cold air was a stark contrast to the hot bar, crammed to capacity.

A large black van idled at the curb. The back passenger door was open. The person pushed me forward, toward the van. I didn't even have enough time to scream for help before I was pushed inside.

POPPY

I landed on the cold floor. The van was empty. I sat, looking for an escape, when a woman with long black hair climbed in. She closed the door and smiled down at me.

"I thought that would be harder," she said, stretching her arms out in front of her. "For being *his*, I'm surprised that was so easy."

Beads of sweat dripped down my forehead. My arms trembled as I pushed myself backward. What did she want with me? Obviously, she had the wrong person.

I opened my mouth, but the woman held up her hand, silencing me with her gaze.

"Save me the speech. I don't need to hear it." She withdrew a long silver knife from her boot. "I guess this means another mark for me," she added, pulling her shirt down to reveal two large tattoos. "Enley will be happy to hear it's done."

My chest tightened. "You have the wrong person. I don't know what you're talking about."

The woman smiled. She knelt, drawing the blade against my throat. My heartbeat thrashed in my ears. I couldn't back up any farther. I was sandwiched between the driver's seat and the backseat, the woman before me. I was trapped.

The oniony smell of sweat filled my nose. The woman leaned into me, pushing my head against the side of the van. She dug the knife deeper into my throat. Dizziness washed over me. I didn't want to die.

I reached up, struggling to push the knife away. My fingers curled around her hands. She straddled me, using her weight to overpower me. When our eyes connected, my stomach coiled. They were narrowed at me, her face expressionless. With one last burst of energy, I brought my knee up, hoping to startle her enough to loosen her hold.

Undeterred, the woman pushed my right hand off her arm, the knife never leaving my throat. My hand fell to the floor, landing on something cold. I curled my fingers around it, dragging it from under the seat.

Adrenaline coursed through me. I raised my makeshift weapon into the air. Before she could stop me, I swung at her. The tire iron connected with her cheek. The woman fell backwards, the knife flying from her hands. I used the time to scramble further away from her, jumping onto the backseat. I scanned the van for the knife, but I couldn't see it. The woman uttered a curse. Before I could move, she pulled the knife from under the driver seat. Her eyes flashed with rage, all aimed at me.

She ran her tongue across her lips. "I'm going to enjoy this."

I crawled toward the door. My fingers reached for the handle too late. The woman grabbed my ankle. She pulled me back to her. I screamed; my lungs frantic for air. I kicked my feet in her direction. She grabbed my hair, pulling strands from the scalp. I screamed again; the pain radiating down my body.

"Please," I said. "You have the wrong person."

"Where the poppy grows, discord sows. The irony…"

For a moment, I stopped struggling, trying to make sense of

what she said. My parents named me Poppy because it was my mother's favorite flower. It wasn't a common name where I lived.

An arm wrapped around my neck. The woman pulled me closer. I struggled, but her grip remained iron tight. I dug my fingernails into her skin. Unfazed, she pressed the blade into my throat. Warm liquid oozed out. I gasped for breath as it cut deeper into the flesh.

My vision blurred. I pictured my parents. I wanted to see them again. One last time, I wanted to tell them I loved them. I wanted to see Addie. This wasn't how I was supposed to die.

Bright light filled my vision. The pressure around my neck disappeared. A weightlessness overtook me. Was this it? Was I dying?

"Poppy?"

My vision refocused, the bright light fading. I wasn't dead. Two muscular arms wrapped around me in a careful and warm embrace. A face came into focus. The man from the bar looked down at me. I inhaled deeply, filling my lungs with fresh oxygen. It felt so good. But I couldn't quite make sense of what had just happened. Where had the woman gone? Who was she? Why had she attacked me? And where did this guy come from?

"I should have come for you sooner."

I met his gaze. Bright blue eyes looked down at me. I struggled in his grasp, but was too weak to move much. My vision blurred again, and I shut my eyes, trying to stifle the panic coursing through me.

"I won't hurt you." He helped me sit up and knelt before me, gently pushing a strand of hair out of my eyes.

I flinched at his touch, and he brought his hand back, rubbing it along his pants. Bright red blood trickled down my chest. My hands flew to my throat, the image of the knife imprinted in my memory. I opened my mouth and pushed the words out painfully, "Where is she?"

He looked down. When he didn't answer, I followed his gaze. The woman was on the floor. Her long black hair covered her face.

"Is she…"

He nodded.

This had to be a terrible dream. I would wake up at any moment, the nightmare soon to be forgotten. I looked away, not wanting to meet his gaze again, and saw blood on my arms. My blood.

"Poppy—"

My fingers gripped the seat cushion. "How do you know my name? Who are you? Why were you in my house?"

"I'm going to take you home," he answered, ignoring my questions.

He stood, turning to the front of the van. My head throbbed with a heartbeat all its own. My body was sore, and I was tired. I wanted to know what was happening and why my life was falling apart around me.

"No," I said. "Answer me. Who are you? Why did she attack me? She wanted to kill me…She knew my name…She said something about poppies and discord."

"Where the poppy grows, discord sows," he said, turning to face me again.

I nodded. "Yeah, what does that mean?"

"I'm going to take you home."

Why wouldn't he give me a straightforward answer? I elongated my back. My muscles protested, tensing against the sudden movement. A cry escaped my lips.

He knelt again, facing me. "Do you remember me? Do I look familiar…at all?"

I narrowed my eyes. Was he being serious? Of course, he looked familiar. He broke into my house.

Before I could answer, he flinched. He leaned forward, gripping the seat around me. His head fell backward, and a deep, guttural scream escaped his lips. The hair on my arms stood on end when I noticed a new tattoo on his neck joining the others. A long, black line slowly appeared, as if rising from his body.

I leaned into the seat, hardly believing what I saw. Worse, I was trapped between his arms. He leaned even closer, his head falling forward. I inhaled his cologne; the woodsy scent surrounded me.

"I thought I had more time before the mark would appear," he muttered.

"I guess this means another mark for me," the woman's words echoed in my head. She had the same tattoos on her chest. She had insinuated that she would receive another mark when she killed me. How was that possible?

He lowered his shirt to look at the mark. I counted the tattoos that snaked up his chest.

Seven.

My stomach lurched. The woman said something about me being *his*. Who was she referring to? The man before me? I summoned all the strength I had left and ducked underneath his arm, pushing him away. My hand clasped the door handle, but before I could open it, he set me back on the seat.

"It's not safe for you out there."

I scooted away from him, blood staining the leather. "Please, I have a family. Just let me go."

He brought his hands to his chest, running his fingers over the new mark. "Poppy, I won't hurt you. We're fated. If anything happened to you..." his words hung in the air.

Fated. Nothing made sense. The ringing in my ears intensified, and I put my head in my hands, trying to think clearly.

"My name's Thaniel," he said, breaking the silence. "We were friends until your parents left our land five years ago. Once the decree was announced."

I shook my head. I'd lived in White Bridge my entire life.

Now I knew, without a shadow of a doubt, he had the wrong girl.

"I'm sorry, I'm not who you think I am," I said. "I've lived in White Bridge my entire life."

He sighed. "No, you haven't. They altered your memories. I'm taking you home—they'll tell you."

"No," I protested, pushing away from him. "You have the wrong person."

"I can prove it." He took my hands and looked into my eyes. "You have a birthmark on your right shoulder. It looks like a heart."

My breath stilled. How did he know that? I hated that birthmark. George used to tell me how ugly it was. I opened my mouth, but nothing came out. My brain worked in overdrive, trying to process everything. It didn't make sense. I would remember moving to White Bridge five years ago. I would remember meeting him, being friends with him.

He exhaled loudly. "I tried to forget you. I wanted to let you live a normal life, away from it all."

"I don't understand." My thoughts were frantic, moving in circles. "Away from what?"

"I'll explain everything later," he said. "I promise. After we ditch the van."

His eyes moved to the body on the floor. He released my hands and climbed into the driver's seat. When the ignition caught, I glanced out the window. Now was my chance to escape, but something held me in the seat. The fact that they knew my name, that he knew about the birthmark, was too much. I needed answers.

Thaniel pulled the van into the road, merging with traffic. I watched McLoughlin's disappear, the lights of the city fading.

THANIEL

$\mathcal{B}$y the time I reached the highway, my anger had abated. While it hadn't gone away completely, my breathing had settled, and my muscles relaxed. That had been too close.

I was going to kill Enley Greymoore.

Through the rearview mirror, I watched Poppy slide closer to the door, her hand resting on the handle. Her dress was wet and even though it was drying, the sweet, sugary smell of soda permeated the air. I had seen the drink spill on her. I had been right behind her. That's when I saw the woman drag her outside.

My insides churned as the image replayed in my head. How much had the woman been paid? The fact that she was Shadow Marked hadn't surprised me. It only meant that she was descended from Marwood, my home. At one time, her family had helped mine.

Our curse was painful—a reminder of the lives my grandfather took when he stole the throne. I was aware that some resented us, and it only made sense that they were working with our enemy.

Poppy moved her head to the right. Her breathing settled as she gazed out the window. A long gash marked her throat. Even though it wasn't deep, it never should have happened. I should have seen the woman. I should have seen her marks. Now that Enley knew where she was, she had to leave.

I was going to take her home, and tell Emilia and Flinn to come back to Marwood, where our army could protect her. Even if Poppy never wanted to be with me, I would still ensure her safety. I would give her the choice—once she had her memories back.

I dug my phone out of my pocket. With my eyes on the road, I dialed Cerros.

He answered after the first ring, "Are you on your way back?"

"Something happened," I answered, meeting Poppy's gaze in the rearview mirror. "I need help disposing of a van...and a body."

Poppy's eyes left mine, turning to the woman on the floor. It was in that moment I realized I should have brought Poppy to the front seat. Or moved the body to the trunk. I hadn't been thinking.

Cerros sighed. "I was going to bed."

"I'll be there in about ten minutes," I said. "I need to take your car. Mine's at McLaughlin's."

His reply was immediate, "The bar?"

"Someone attacked her." I brought the phone to my left ear and lowered my voice, "The woman was Shadow Marked."

"I'll see you in ten."

When the dial tone hit my ear, I let off the gas pedal. I slowed to make a right onto Paulson Avenue when the front tire hit a curb. While Cerros and I had learned how to drive, the van was bigger than anything I had ever driven before. Not to mention my nerves were making it hard to concentrate.

Poppy leaned forward. I wanted to say something, anything, but the words wouldn't come. I had imagined this moment for five years, ever since she disappeared. Now that it was here, I couldn't think straight.

She turned back to the window, her face stoic. I could only imagine she was trying to process everything. A drop of blood fell from her nose. Instinctively, she ran her hand above her lips.

"Where are you taking me?"

I tore my gaze from the rearview mirror. "After we drop the van off, I'm taking you home."

She nodded. "Will you answer my questions?"

I bit my lip. I had told her I would answer her questions. She deserved to know the truth. "Yes."

"The tattoo. It seemed to come out of your skin."

How was I going to explain my family's curse? It was the reason her parents left after the decree. I had to tread lightly. "Not now. When you're safe, I'll answer your questions."

She placed her head against the window. For everything that happened, she seemed calm. Maybe deep down she recognized me, knew I wouldn't hurt her.

I wasn't sure if I was ready to tell her the truth. After she learned about my curse, maybe she wouldn't want anything to do with me. The one thing I knew for certain was that I wasn't willing to lose her. I had tried multiple times to forget her, to let her live a normal life, but it never lasted long. The pull was always there.

Besides the death marks—the tattoos that appeared with every life we take—we're fated to one partner. No one else could ever fulfill the void. Poppy was mine, but if she chose someone else, I would have to be okay with it. While my family was subjected to the curse, our fated weren't. They could find happiness with others.

My uncle's fated married another. He died two years later.

My father told me he died in his sleep, a random, unfortunate coincidence. I knew better.

He died of a broken heart.

POPPY

Another drop of blood fell from my nose, landing on my chest. I didn't have to look to know that my outfit was ruined. My throat ached where the woman ran the blade across my skin. Thankfully, it hadn't cut too deep.

Thaniel slowed the van before making a right onto a dirt road. A slick black car appeared, idling on the shoulder. The driver's door opened, and a man stepped out. Thaniel parked the van before unrolling the window.

The man approached the driver's side and crossed his arms over his chest. "You owe me."

"The body's in the backseat," Thaniel answered.

The man stepped back as Thaniel opened his door. They continued talking, every so often glancing in my direction. I watched their exchange, wishing I could hear what they were saying.

Another drop of blood slid down my lips. I flinched at the copper taste. My eyes darted to the dead woman. Even though she had been trying to kill me, a twinge of guilt reverberated through me.

The door to my right opened, and Thaniel held his hand out,

offering to help me. Even in the dark, his markings were visible. I didn't know if I could fully trust him, but I needed answers.

I stepped out of the van. My body was sore, my muscles tight. When I was standing, I pulled my hand out of his. His eyes ran across me, as if making sure I was okay.

The other man appeared, stepping around the back. He had the same vivid blue eyes as Thaniel, but his hair was short. Without looking at me, he peered into the backseat. "I'll take care of this. Keys are in the car." The man closed the door. "I'll call you when I'm finished."

Thaniel led me across the street, toward the black car. He opened the passenger door. I stepped backward, my adrenaline spiking.

"You can trust me." He leaned close. "I'm taking you home."

He did save my life. And I wanted answers. I slid inside the car, my bare legs sticking to the leather.

He walked around the front, finally stepping into the driver's side. After fastening his seatbelt, he glanced at me, making sure mine was buckled before stepping on the gas. The dashboard lights illuminated his face, revealing a tiny freckle on his right cheek.

When I couldn't take the silence any longer, I asked, "Who are you?"

He merged onto the highway. His silence hung over us, igniting the anger inside me. I settled into the seat, watching him out of the corner of my eye. As much as I wanted to scream, to demand an answer, he needed to concentrate. We didn't need to get into a car accident.

"Do you even know how to get to my house?" As soon as the words were out of my mouth, I regretted them. Of course, he knew the way. He had been there earlier.

He didn't answer, as if knowing I caught my mistake. At least he didn't acknowledge it.

"What were you doing in my house?" I asked. "I thought it

was stress…school has been hard…my boyfriend broke up with me." I couldn't stop the words. I shook my head. He didn't need to know any of this. I didn't even know him.

"He's a fool."

That wasn't the answer I expected. I turned back to him. He tore his gaze from the road, looking at me.

"Your boyfriend's a fool."

I pinched the bridge of my nose. "Ex-boyfriend."

He turned away, his gaze on the road once more. When he didn't answer my question, I turned toward the window, looking inside the cars we passed. Normal people with normal problems. What I wouldn't give for a normal Friday night.

"I was checking on you," he finally answered.

I turned from the window. "Why? Why would you want to check on a stranger? I'm not who you think I am."

"I know about your birthmark," he said.

That detail still nagged at me. How had he known about that? Depending on how long he had been watching me, maybe he had seen me in a tank top. I sighed. "Lucky guess."

Thaniel turned on the blinker, merging into the right lane to exit the highway. "Your parents will confirm everything. I'm surprised they let you out of the house tonight."

I rubbed my forehead, trying to push back the headache. "When they tell you they don't know who you are, and don't know what you're talking about, will you leave us alone?"

"They won't, but sure."

I wished I had my cell phone. I could have just called them, put them on speaker and asked them. Or called the police. But then I would be no closer to the answers I needed.

Thaniel slowed the car. I looked up to find we were at a stoplight. My mind raced. Would he really just leave when my parents told him he had the wrong girl?

My stomach sank. What if he was telling the truth? What if

my parents had secrets of their own? A moment later, the car lurched forward.

"A thank you would be nice."

I turned to face him again. "Thank you? You mean thank you for stalking me?"

He smiled. "I saved your life."

I sank back into the seat. My hand flew to my throat, and I flinched when my fingers touched the wound. What was that man going to do with her body and the van?

"Who was that? The man back there?"

"My brother," he answered.

"Does your brother have a name?"

"You're full of questions," his voice was flat. "His name's Cerros."

"I suppose I have a lot of questions," I said. "For someone whose life is being turned upside down."

He turned into my development, slowing the car. I was relieved to see my house. He parked at the curb. I reached down to unbuckle my seatbelt, my body protesting each move. When I looked up, Thaniel was at my door. He opened it, offering me his hand again. I pushed him away, standing on my own, using the excitement of finally being home to fuel me.

He closed the door behind me, and I made my way to the front porch. The lights were on, which meant my parents were still up. Thaniel ran ahead of me. He dashed up the stairs, taking them two at a time. At the front door, he stopped. He turned back to me, and I saw what had caught his attention.

A windowpane near the handle had shattered. My heart raced.

He reached into his pocket and withdrew his knife. He held it out, waving me forward. "Stay at my side."

I nodded. He pushed open the door, and I took a deep breath.

Inside, silence met us.

POPPY

Thaniel's boots crunched on the broken glass. Each step sent a shiver down my spine. An emptiness settled in my stomach and my legs trembled. I stepped forward, taking it all in. The ottoman was across the room, a recliner was on its side, and the coffee table was tipped over.

The house was quiet, everything still. Thaniel led me to the dining room, but it was in the same disarray as the living room. The dining table chairs were on their sides, the flower center-piece broken, water had spilled onto the table and warped the wood. I ran into the kitchen.

The backdoor was open; the mail was strewn on the floor.

"Mom? Dad?"

No one answered.

I ran past Thaniel, back into the dining room and up the stairs. The bathroom was empty. I sprinted to my parents' room. The door was shut. Before I could open it, Thaniel was by my side. He held his finger to his lips and leaned close. My heartbeat quickened. I couldn't make sense of the jumbled thoughts swirling in my head.

He gripped the doorknob, slowly turning it to the right. I

held my breath, imagining my parents on the other side of the door with a logical explanation for the mess downstairs. The door swung open easily.

Silence met us. The room was empty.

I ran back into the hall. There was one more place to look. My bedroom. It was the last place we hadn't searched.

When I stepped inside, my stomach fell. It looked exactly as it had when I left with Addie. Textbooks covered the desk. My bed was made, the comforter tightly pressed into the mattress. My makeup littered the vanity. The mirror reflected a stranger covered in dirt and blood; her dress ripped.

I took another slow step into the room, my eyes on the mirror, taking in my appearance. I placed a hand under my nose, wiping the dried blood. Thaniel appeared behind me, and I lost it. The tears came before I could stop them. My parents would never leave the house in such disarray. I sank to the ground, my legs too weak to hold me. My eyes stung, the tears mixing with mascara. I couldn't seem to catch my breath, and my head throbbed. Thaniel's footsteps carried as he left the room, leaving me to my breakdown. I brought my knees to my chest, placing my head on them. This couldn't be real. Maybe it was all a dream, a terrible nightmare I just had to wake from.

When Thaniel entered the room again, he knelt in front of me. He placed a wet washcloth in my hands.

"Thank you," I said.

"We need to go. It isn't safe here."

My hands fell to my lap. "I have nowhere else to go."

"With me," he said. "Pack a bag."

I shook my head. "I don't even know you."

He took my arm, bringing me close. "You're going with me, one way or another. Pack a bag. We don't have time."

I pulled my arm out of his grip. "You can't tell me what to do. I'm going to my friend's. She has my cellphone. Maybe my parents tried to call me."

An idea sprang to mind.

I ran out of the room; the washcloth forgotten. Addie had my cellphone, but if I dialed my number, I could listen to the voicemails. I flew down the stairs, my momentum carrying me so fast I almost ran into the wall.

We still had a landline. It was in the kitchen, hardly used. I lifted the phone off the receiver. The harsh dial tone was like music to my ears. I quickly entered my number. By the second ring, Thaniel had joined me.

Before my voicemail could connect, someone answered, "Poppy?"

A weight lifted off my shoulders. "Addie, this is important. Are there any messages from my parents on my phone?"

A harsh wail met my ears, and my stomach sank. Something was wrong.

She took a deep breath. "He wants me to tell you something," her voice was trembling. "He has your parents. He's coming for you."

My ears rang. Had I heard right? Who had my parents? Who was coming for me? My hands trembled, and I nearly dropped the phone. "Addie, who's coming for me?"

"He wants to talk to you."

"Who wants to talk to me?" I screamed into the phone. "Addie, please!"

Thaniel took the phone. The room spun as he turned away, speaking calmly, "What do you want?"

I couldn't hear the answer, but his face paled. A moment later, he placed the phone on the receiver. "We're going."

Before I could respond, he grabbed my hand, bringing me to the backdoor and onto the porch. I pulled away from him, but he wouldn't release me. My breath hitched. I needed a moment to clear my head. I had to figure out what was happening. Trying to break free, I swung my arm at him.

He spun around, his eyes meeting mine. "Poppy, I'll tell you everything. Anything you want. But first, we need to go. Your life's in danger."

He wasn't making sense. Why would my life be in danger? I was a college student. A normal twenty-one-year-old.

"You need to trust me," he added. "I'm trying to protect you. We'll save your family, but first we need to leave."

"You'll help me find them?" I asked, my voice cracking. "We need to call the police."

Thaniel ran a hand through his hair. "The police can't help us. You can't stay here. He knows where you are. We don't have much time."

"Who?" I asked. "None of this makes sense. You all have the wrong girl, the wrong family. There's no reason anyone would want me."

"Trust me," he said, "I promise I'll tell you everything."

My body trembled, my legs like jelly. The night was silent as I contemplated my options. I looked back at my house, a memory flashing before me. Before I left with Addie, my father asked my mother if I should stay home. After the events of the evening, her response took a whole new meaning.

"She's fine. The new moon already passed."

My eyes flew upward, searching the sky. While the new moon had already passed, it had only been a few nights ago. A shiver went through me, running from my neck to my toes. My parents knew more than they were letting on.

They had secrets of their own. Secrets that may be our undoing.

THANIEL

$\mathcal{E}$nley Greymoore had Poppy's parents.

I cracked my knuckles, imagining all the things I was going to do to him. It had surprised me to hear his voice on the other end of the phone. I had been expecting her friend. His voice had been cold, devoid of the usual hatred he reserved for me. Our families were enemies, all stemming from a decades-long feud over the throne.

My grandfather, James Ashton, stumbled upon Marwood by accident. He worked on his family's farm in northern Pennsylvania, the same land that Poppy's parents were hiding in—only they chose upstate New York. He had been out with his friends, partying in the woods, when he leaned against a large oak tree, the new moon high above him.

When he found himself just outside of Marwood, he thought he had been dreaming, drunk even. He hid in the stables, learning what he could about the world around him. By the time the next new moon came around, he had pieced together what he could about traveling through the dimensions. He found the oak tree and traveled back to his home in Pennsylvania, where he gathered an army to overthrow the king, claiming the throne for himself. Naturally, the Greymoores hated us, going so far as to setting the curse upon us.

I balled my fingers into my palms, trying to ground myself from a feud I had nothing to do with. I scanned the tree line.

Poppy brought her arms to her chest, rubbing her hands over the skin. Tiny goosebumps dotted her flesh. She should have changed out of that dress. I remembered seeing a jacket on the kitchen floor. We had stepped over it on our way to the backdoor.

I scanned our surroundings once more. When I was satisfied that no one was near, I turned to her. "I'll be right back. Don't move."

Her eyes widened. "Where are you going?"

I paused, a lightness washing over me. She didn't want me to leave. Before I lost myself in the feeling, I stepped away. "I'm getting you a jacket."

She nodded; her eyes were vacant. She sat on the porch steps, her head trained on the night sky. Against everything in my better judgment, I stepped forward. I wanted to comfort her. But I was only a stranger.

In the distance, a dog howled, and I came to my senses. Now was our chance to leave. I had to get her to safety. I hadn't come this far only to lose her.

Poppy turned to face me. "Am I dreaming? This can't be real."

My stomach sank. How was I going to answer? This never should have happened. I had let her down. I should have known Enley was in White Bridge.

"Stay here," I said. "I'll be right back."

She turned, her gaze on the sky once more.

I ran inside. As much as I didn't want to leave her outside, if she came in with me, she would want to pack. We didn't have time. I was sure Enley was on his way.

The jacket was on the floor next to the door. I scanned the

kitchen, looking for anything out of place, a clue to what happened. Instinctively, I turned, as if connected to Poppy. When I found her still sitting on the porch steps, I bent to retrieve the jacket, eager to be on our way.

When the phone rang, a chill went down my spine. My body tensed at each shrill ring. I snagged the jacket and sprinted out the door.

I was taking Poppy home.

When Thaniel reappeared, my father's jacket was in his hands. He tossed it to me. I caught it easily, wrapping it around my shoulders. The fleece was warm on my skin, but I wished it covered my legs. "I need to change."

He closed the door. "There's no time."

He walked past me, down the steps. I stood. My stomach fluttered, another reminder that my life had veered very off track.

As I made my way down the steps, I caught the scent of my father's cologne on the jacket. My legs grew weak, and I nearly tripped. Thaniel bypassed the driveway and made his way into the woods that bordered my house. I paused at the line, watching him cross the forest threshold. A gust of wind blew past us, and I shivered.

"We don't have to walk," I called. "If you don't want to take your brother's car, we can take mine."

He didn't stop as he said, "Where we're going, we don't need a car."

I turned the options in my head. I had nowhere else to go, no one else to trust. I needed to find my family. I was caught up in something dangerous; Thaniel as well. I didn't even have my cell phone.

Another cold gust of wind blew past me, and I hurried to catch up with him. I threw my hands in my jacket pockets, trying to warm them. We walked in silence. My feet ached, and I wished I had thought to change into sneakers. My once near-perfect ballet flats were now torn.

When he stopped, I caught up with him, exhaling loudly. We were almost at the end of the property. Beyond the patch of woods that comprised our five-acre yard, another housing development sat.

"I'm beginning to question my decision to trust you," I said. "Is your plan to hide in my backyard?"

"I need to find a tree," he answered. "It has to be an older one, not one of these newer ones," he added, pointing to a small tree to his left.

I didn't think I heard him right. He couldn't be serious.

He seemed to sense my confusion. "Trust me."

"That's a big ask," I said. "I just met you."

"No, you didn't. I already told you we're friends." He stopped. "We *were* friends."

It was my turn to chuckle. "We must not have been very good friends if I don't remember you."

He looked away, his eyes studying the merits of each tree. Since I wasn't sure what we were looking for, I used the time to steady my breathing. My mind ran over the events of the night. Who had Addie and my parents? Thaniel seemed to know who it was. His face had paled when he was on the phone.

He pointed to a large tree near the end of the property. "That one should work."

I slowly followed. He walked up to the tree, his long legs easily traversing the rough ground. He closed his eyes. The air shimmered as he whispered something under his breath. I stepped backward, caught off guard, and tripped over a tree root.

He opened his eyes. "Ready?"

I stood, brushing the dirt off my blood-stained dress. "For what?"

"We're going home."

He placed his hand on the knotty trunk, only instead of touching the bark, it went through it. His hand vanished.

A low scream escaped my lips.

He turned to me, pulling his hand out of the tree. "It's just a portal."

I stepped forward, doubting what I had seen. Perhaps it was a trick of the light. There's no way I had seen his hand disappear.

"Home?" I asked. "Your home's inside a tree?"

He shook his head. "No, our home is *through* the tree."

My legs trembled and my stomach coiled. I couldn't make sense of his answer. He was crazy. This wasn't possible. He was playing with me. Was this all a cruel joke? "You can't be serious," the words tumbled out of my mouth.

He held my gaze. "You were born in Marwood. When my decree was made public, your parents left. I think they were trying to protect you."

My skin tingled at his words. "Protect me?"

He nodded. "From me."

I shook my head, the words not making sense. "I don't understand."

"Trust me, Poppy."

I shook my head. "You're just as crazy as that woman was."

He bridged the gap between us, taking my hands in his. I quickly yanked them out of his grasp.

"Don't touch me," I said, my voice a whisper. "You've killed people."

His eyes bore into mine. "I have. I would do it again."

My pulse quickened. Was this his plan? Did he bring me all the way out here to kill me?

"I've only killed those who threaten me... and the people I love."

My mind raced. "You killed that woman. In the van. Were you following me to get to her?"

He looked away. Silence hung between us.

I couldn't stay with him. My legs propelled me forward, my shoes digging into my heels. This had been a mistake. If I could just make it out of the tree line, I could make a run for my neighbors.

A hand gripped my shoulders, and I tripped. I stumbled to the ground, landing on my knees. The adrenaline coursing through me dulled the pain, and I scrambled back onto my feet.

Thaniel bent, holding me still. "Poppy, please. I'm not going to hurt you. I killed that woman because she threatened someone I love. You. You don't remember, but try. Hurting you would kill me."

Tears streamed down my cheeks. No matter how hard I tried, I couldn't catch my breath. He picked me up, cradling me in his arms. I tried to escape his grip, but he was too strong.

"I'm sorry," he whispered. "I'll tell you more when we're safe. When we get back to Marwood, your memories should return. I'm going to help you find your family."

He picked up his pace, sprinting toward the tree. I braced myself for impact, shielding my head in his chest. But instead of hitting the tree trunk, we effortlessly slid through it.

When we crossed the threshold, Thaniel set me down. We were in another forest, only this wasn't my backyard. Large, bright fireflies lit up the darkness, illuminating the copper-tinted leaves of the surrounding trees. The grass was the palest shade of green. A soft breeze curled around me. The sweetest scent of honey and vanilla filled me. I spun in a circle, taking it all in.

"Where are we?"

Thaniel placed his hands in his pockets. "Renathria. Our home in Marwood is about an hour's walk. Do you think you can handle it?"

My mind spun. I couldn't process that we had stepped into a tree in my backyard, and now we were in a new world. My hands trembled. I wrapped them around my chest, hoping to settle the anxious energy. "I don't even know what to say," I whispered.

His eyes scanned the forest. "You'll be safe here. I have resources in Marwood to help us find your family. When we find them, I'll leave you alone. I'll make sure you're safe, but you'll never have to see me again." His eyes met mine. "Unless you want."

The large fireflies danced around us. They were beautiful. When I saw the tree we had stepped out from, I slowly inched toward it. The bark was rough, with large knots in the trunk. The shiny copper-colored leaves fluttered in the wind. Bright red fruit dangled from the branches.

"How did we get here?"

"Old magic," he answered.

I narrowed my eyes.

He continued, "Nature magic is the most powerful magic we have. I drew on the tree's life force. The older the tree, the more life force."

I didn't understand. Magic wasn't real. That was reserved for TV or books. I bit my lips. An image of the tattoo appearing on him overwhelmed me. How could I explain that? How could I explain stepping into the tree and leaving my backyard?

"Will you answer my questions now?"

"I will," he answered. "Although it may be better to let the memories come first."

I didn't even hesitate. "No. I need answers. Who has my parents and Addie? What do they want from me?"

He began walking. "The Greymoores have them. To be specific, Enley Greymoore has them."

"Why? What does he want with them?"

He shook his head. His gaze shifted forward. "He doesn't want them, per se. He wants to hurt me. The easiest way to do that is to go after what's mine—my fated."

I kept my gaze in front of me, not wanting to disturb the moment. I was finally getting the answers I needed.

"What does that mean?" I asked. "Your fated?"

He walked ahead of me, moving a tree branch out of the path. "Let me start from the beginning. I'm Shadow Marked. My family is. It's our curse."

"The tattoos?" I asked, wondering what that had to do with his fated. "Who cursed you? Why?"

His hand flew to the marks on his chest. "The Greymoores cursed us after my grandfather took the throne from them. If we kill someone, the tattoos appear, a reminder of the blood we spilled, the lives we've taken."

If I hadn't seen the marks appear, I wouldn't have believed it. His story sounded like the plot of a fantasy novel. Magical curses didn't make sense in my well-ordered world, but neither did walking into trees and traveling to other lands. His answer struck me, as if finally picking up what he had meant to gloss over.

I turned to him. "The throne? Are you—"

"I'll never be king," he answered quickly. "My brother Cerros will."

My thoughts raced, unpacking the implications of what he'd told me. He was a prince. What did he want with me? "Is there a way to stop the curse?"

He shook his head. "Not that we can figure out. It's passed down through our line."

I nodded, as if what he was saying made a shred of sense. When I woke up this morning, I was an average college student, trying to make sense of Shakespeare. Now I was just as confused, only it was life or death.

"How does your fated come into this?" I asked, trying to connect the pieces he was sharing. "Is it part of the curse?"

"Yes," he answered. "Part of the curse is that we're fated with one other person. My people go through a decree. It's when our magmar—our wise woman—senses our pairings. The person we're meant to be with in this lifetime, the person we're bound to."

I frowned, trying to make sense of the curse. How could having a fated—someone bound to you—be a curse? It seemed like that would be a blessing—knowing there was someone out there to love you.

"That doesn't seem like a curse," I said.

He rubbed the back of his neck before looking at me again. "You would think. Our fated usually isn't one of our people. It's someone who's not cursed, someone who doesn't feel the same pull, someone who has free will. They don't have to proceed with the decree, they can move on, find someone else to live their life with."

"So, you can move on as well?"

He looked away. "How do you move on from your soulmate?"

I had never believed in the concept of soulmates. It didn't make sense. Life was too random, too unpredictable for it to work. What if your soulmate was born in a completely different country? What if there was a massive age difference?

He stopped beside me. "You don't believe in soulmates?"

"No," I answered. "If you're truly soulmates, why would your fated not love you in return?"

"A lot of reasons." He sighed. "Free will. Circumstances out of our control. The simple fact that we're cursed is enough to scare anyone away."

I ducked underneath a tree branch. "But what does this all have to do with me? With my family?"

"I went through my decree at seventeen," he answered.

My stomach twisted. I knew where this was going. He already told me I was his fated.

"It's you, Poppy," he whispered. "Our magmar told me you're my fated. That's why your parents left. Honestly, I can't blame them."

My head spun. If what he was saying was true, then why couldn't I remember anything? If we were truly soulmates, why couldn't I recognize the stranger before me? "Why would my parents leave?" I asked. "You're a prince. That sounds like every parent's dream."

He scoffed. "Not my family. We wear our kills for all to see."

I swallowed. That was valid. I could see my parents having a problem with that. In fact, I had a problem with that. I didn't even know if I could fully trust him. He had seven marks on his chest. "Does your family…kill for fun? Is it a sport for you?"

He began walking again. "No. But we all have marks, all except my sister."

"Who did you kill?"

He stopped walking again. "I'm a trained fighter, Poppy. I work with our army. They've all been in self-defense, all except tonight. She was going to kill you."

While it was nice to know he had only killed in self-defense, I was still unsettled. He was a stranger. A stranger who thought I was his soulmate.

I balled my fists, anger rising inside my stomach. My life was crumbling around me, one layer at a time, all because of a feud over a kingdom. I was angry for my parents. For Addie. She was innocent in all of this.

"You said you'd help me find my family," I said, my brain sorting through the jumbled thoughts. "Then you'd leave me alone. If we're truly fated, why are you so willing to give me up? Oh, and how did you even find me?"

The fireflies waned, disappearing into the night.

He exhaled, his eyes meeting mine. "We're connected. I found you so easily because of our bond. Your parents didn't realize how deep it was."

"And you're willing to give it up? That bond?"

His nostrils flared, his jaw set. "If that's what you want. I won't force it on you. You're not bound to the decree. We are fated, though. I imagine you'll begin feeling it soon. But if you want me to leave, if you want to spend your life with someone like George, I won't stand in your way."

Did I want to spend my life with someone like George? Images of him dancing in McLaughlin's flashed in my mind. He leaned into his date, his mouth brushing against hers. I didn't want that. "Why do I have memories from my childhood…in White Bridge? I really think you have the wrong person."

"Those aren't real," he answered softly. "Your parents must have paid someone to give you those memories. In time, you'll see."

I shook my head. "My parents wouldn't do that to me."

He shrugged. "How can you be so sure? You don't think your parents would do whatever they could to protect you from a family of killers?"

He turned forward, leaving me to ponder his question. How could I be so sure? If everything he said was true, could I even trust my parents?

When we reached a large trail lined with iridescent wildflowers, I paused. Their stems glowed, lighting the way. Another reminder that I was in over my head.

I wrapped my jacket tighter around my chest. The only thing I knew for certain was that I was going to find my family. I was going home. With or without my memories.

POPPY

e had been walking for so long my legs ached. Every step brought additional pain. Blisters covered my feet from my ballet flats. Occasionally, I would glance at Thaniel. It didn't look as if he was bothered at all. His long legs easily traversed the path, and he seemed to know the route fairly well. When a tree branch was in our path, he would hold it so I could pass.

Our silence gave me ample time to think about my childhood, replaying every memory. When I was eight, I fell off my bike and skinned my knee. I remember it so clearly because my neighbor Chad had been outside. He was a year older than me, and I had the biggest crush on him.

My tenth birthday flashed through my head. My parents had decorated our house in pink and purple streamers. When I came home from school, they popped purple confetti as I walked through the door.

I remembered our family vacation to the Outer Banks when I was twelve. I swam in the ocean, collected seashells, and built sandcastles with my father. Were these memories lies?

Even though my parents had secrets, secrets that affected

me, I missed them terribly. I tried to remember the last words I had said to them. Had I told them I loved them? Did they know I loved them? I stifled a cry as the memories overwhelmed me.

My thoughts shifted to Addie. Was she scared? Was she with my parents? Or were they separated? How had she gotten caught up in all of this? She had been in a crowded bar. When I left, she had been on the dance floor, surrounded by people. Had she been taken when I left for the bathroom?

I broke our silence, "After seeing George, and then you, I went looking for Addie. She wasn't where I left her. She may have already been taken when the woman attacked me. Could they have been in the bar?"

Thaniel shrugged. "I would have seen Enley, but that doesn't mean he hadn't hired someone to take her. The woman I killed was working for him."

A low howl echoed around us. He stopped walking, listening to the sounds of the forest. I had been naïve to think that the woods were safe. We weren't in my backyard anymore.

When another low howl sounded, closer than the last, Thaniel froze.

I couldn't see anything in the dark, and there were no fire-flies or iridescent flowers to give us light. A branch snapped and my stomach dropped.

"Run," he whispered. "I'll be behind you."

Another snarl sounded.

I didn't even answer. I took off, pushing through the pain. I darted through branches and brambles, running faster than I had ever run before. My lungs burned.

Behind me, something was chasing us, tearing through the trees. Sweat pooled down my face, but I kept moving. When the path dwindled, eventually ending at a large, wide-open field, I stopped.

Thaniel ran into me, catching me when I stumbled forward. "Keep moving."

Behind us, something emerged from the tree line, visible from the light of the moon. My heart exploded, as if trying to escape from my chest. A large cat-like animal covered in thick black fur stalked out of the forest. It was the size of an enormous bear. It gracefully placed one foot in front of the other, its eyes narrowed on its prey—which happened to be us. A pale pink tongue darted out of its mouth, slowly licking its lips in anticipation.

Thaniel ran, pulling me after him. We hadn't made it far before the creature pounced, jumping over us.

"Go." He pushed me away. "It'll chase me. They're hunters."

The creature stepped forward, licking its lips again. Its beady yellow eyes narrowed, watching us. Its leg muscles tensed, preparing to attack. I couldn't outrun that.

Thaniel pushed me again. I stumbled over my feet but kept my balance. He ran away from me. The creature didn't even hesitate. It pounced, following him. When I came to my senses, I darted to my right. I willed my legs faster, ignoring every ounce of pain that hit me.

I had almost made it to the tree line when my foot sank into a divot. My ankle twisted, and I fell forward. I landed in the grass, the wind knocked out of me. For a moment, I forgot where I was and what I was running from.

"Poppy!"

I rolled over, remembering everything. The ground beneath me rumbled, and I sat. Across the field, the black cat-like creature charged, abandoning Thaniel. I scrambled to my feet, but the beast was fast. It was before me in an instant, eyeing me hungrily. I backed up slowly, my body shaking. The creature held up a paw and brought it down. The sharp nails just missed my skin. I crouched, shielding my head.

Thaniel was in front of me in an instant. He jumped on the animal's back. The beast growled, angrily shaking its head from side to side in an attempt to loosen his hold. He held his knife high in the air before bringing it down.

Blood poured out of the wound as he continued to stab, removing and then inserting the knife again and again. Black fur floated to the ground, reminding me of softly falling snow. Moments later, the beast fell lifelessly at my feet.

Thaniel withdrew his knife, wiping the blood on the creature's fur. "That's twice."

My eyes met his. Twice? What did that mean?

"I saved your life twice now," he added. "You owe me."

My gaze drifted back to the body at my feet. He had saved my life twice. I shivered, wondering what owing him would entail.

POPPY

Thaniel placed the knife in his jacket as if nothing happened. Wisps of blond hair framed his face, having fallen out during the scuffle. I shifted on my feet, the adrenaline still coursing through me.

"You ready?" he asked, his eyes moving to mine. "We're almost there."

I opened my mouth, but nothing came out. Everything was happening too fast. The events of the night had been more than I could bear.

Another piece of black fur floated by me, carried in the wind. I sank to the ground. Faint rays of light colored the sky, reminding me of pictures I had seen of the aurora borealis. Everything was different here. I wanted to go back to White Bridge. I wanted my parents to be okay. I wanted to finish the semester.

"Are you hurt?"

I shook my head. "No."

Thaniel knelt before me, placing his hand underneath my chin. When our eyes met, his lips parted. "If you're worried about owing me, don't be. I promise you'll enjoy it."

My breath caught in my throat. What did that mean? I backed away.

He laughed. "It's a joke, Poppy."

I crossed my arms over my chest. "That's not funny."

He stood. "When your memories come back, you'll remember our jokes."

"The elusive memories." I scoffed. "What if they don't? What if they're gone for good?"

He ran a hand through his hair, pushing the loose pieces from his face. I bit my lips, waiting for him to answer, waiting to see if he thought it was possible. Maybe the memories were gone forever, replaced with lies that I was just supposed to live with.

"They'll come back," he finally answered. "They have to."

I stood, my eyes drifting to the black cat-like creature. "Are there more?"

"Yes," he answered simply. "We should go."

A low howl met my ears, and I froze. Were more on their way? Were other creatures tracking us? I waved him forward. "After you."

He placed his hands in his pockets and began walking. I followed, hoping we were almost to the city. I didn't think I could handle much more. I removed my jacket and wrapped it around my waist.

My stomach rumbled, and I realized I hadn't eaten anything since lunch yesterday. I had been too unnerved to eat dinner last night with my parents, not to mention Addie had arrived right at 8, eager to start the night at McLaughlin's.

I used our silence to imagine where we were going in the city. What would it look like? Who would I stay with? Did Thaniel have his own place? Did he live in a castle? Was that where he was taking me? "Who will I stay with when we get there?"

He looked back. "Me."

I gulped. "Do you have your own place?"

The corners of his lips pulled up in a sly smile. "Yes." When I was quiet, he continued, "You'll have your own space. I don't think we'll be there too long."

"Thank you," I said. "For helping me."

"I mean it, Poppy. We'll find them."

I didn't know if it was the warm night or delirium, but the sound of rushing water met my ears. At the noise, my mouth dried. My tongue was heavy, and I longed for something to drink.

Thaniel kept walking, seemingly oblivious to the sound. I was so thirsty the thought of bypassing the water was painful.

"Can we stop? I hear water. I'm so thirsty."

"The river is through that bend," he said, pointing to a cluster of trees. "We'll stop, but only for a moment. We're close."

My calves cramped from all the walking. I ran a hand down my blood-stained dress, trying to smooth the wrinkles. In my head, I knew it didn't make sense. The dress was ruined. No amount of cleaning solution would help. I shouldn't even care about it at this point. I had been through so much; my appearance was the least of my worries.

When we finally crested the hill, the river appeared. I ran, eager for a drink. When I reached the riverbank, I bent and threw my hands in. The crystal-clear water was chilly, and I splashed some on my hands, wiping the dirt and blood off.

"Make sure you drink from an area that has good flow," he said, appearing behind me. "Over there's suitable."

I looked up. He was pointing to an area further down the bank. As hard as it was, I stood and made my way to the spot. The last thing I needed was to get sick from contaminated river water.

"We used to play in this river," he added. "When the heat got unbearable, we would swim in it."

I dipped my hands in the water, the cold spreading up my

arms. At his tone, I couldn't help but wonder what it was like to have a history with someone who didn't even remember you. To be the safeguard of all the forgotten memories. A glance at Thaniel told me all I needed to know.

It was heartbreaking.

THANIEL

I had to prepare for a life without Poppy.

I wasn't sure how long it would take to regain her memories. Would they come all at once, or trickle in slowly? Like a punch to the gut, I realized she may be back in White Bridge before they even came. She may never remember me, and I had to accept that.

I couldn't prolong her time in Marwood. I was going to help her rescue her family, and we couldn't wait. Every day they were with the Greymoores was dangerous.

My stomach roiled at the thought of Enley and his followers. A part of me understood why he was angry, why he hated our family, but the whole feud seemed pointless. His family would never reclaim the throne. He would never be king. Now that he had made his move on Poppy, I had my sights aimed at him. He was playing a dangerous game, one that he was going to lose.

Poppy sat at the edge of the river, scrubbing the blood and dirt off her skin. She angled her head to the side, revealing the long gash on her neck. For a moment, I froze. It had only been a flesh wound, but it was enough to draw my wrath. To calm the anger, I used the moment to scan our surroundings.

One thing I learned from my time with the army was that you could never let your guard down. That's a deadly mistake. My fingers automatically went to my chest, tracing the first mark I ever received.

It had happened on my first overnight assignment. We had been training in the caverns outside of Marwood. It should have been a straightforward mission. Instead, it had triggered my curse.

My friend Luca and I had just settled in for the night. We had spent the day running drills. As the evening wore on, everyone had fallen asleep. We hadn't even heard them attack. I had awoken to find Luca next to me, his throat slit. Bright red blood poured from the wound; his eyes eerily vacant. The only good thing about his death was he hadn't seen it coming.

Besides Luca, we had lost three others. A small fraction of rogues had attacked us, those who claimed no home. They wandered the land, stealing what they could.

I'll never forget looking up from Luca's silent and still body, only to come face to face with the man who had done it. I hadn't even hesitated. I reached for the knife I kept on my belt and plunged it into his chest. He hadn't had time to defend himself. I could still smell the blood.

I never thought I would activate my curse. I never envisioned the marks appearing. I always thought killing someone would have been harder. In reality, it was easy—too easy.

Especially if it was to protect someone I loved.

POPPY

When the large stone fence came into view, I searched my mind, trying to pull out a memory. Moments ago, Thaniel had told me we were near Marwood. We would come upon the backside of the castle—his home. The stone fence didn't look familiar at all. Neither did the guard's post. I frowned, wondering how long the memories would stay hidden.

Thaniel waved his hands in the air. "Cullen."

A young guard appeared atop the fence. "Back from another of your adventures, Prince Thaniel?"

I glanced at Thaniel, finally coming to terms that he was a prince. Even though he had told me, a part of me hadn't quite believed him. Hearing the guard call him a prince confirmed at least part of his story was true.

"I'll be back out before you know it," Thaniel said. "Can you open the gate?"

Cullen climbed down from his post. When the guard's feet landed on solid ground, he faced Thaniel and bowed. Even though he didn't acknowledge me, I could tell he was curious. He was trying too hard to avoid eye contact.

"My father's retired for the night?" Thaniel asked.

Cullen nodded. "Yes."

"My brother?" Thaniel asked.

"You just missed him."

Cullen opened the large wood door, allowing us to pass. When we were inside, Thaniel helped him lock it. Cullen placed his foot on the ladder, ready to climb back to his post.

"Come see me tomorrow," Thaniel said. "I may need your help."

Cullen bowed. "Have a good night."

We walked through the enormous field. I squinted my eyes, trying to see in the dark. Even though the moon and stars provided some light, it was still hard to make out the finer details.

In the distance, a large building appeared. Dark shadows crept forward, consuming everything within their reach. I gasped when I realized it was the castle. Large turrets flanked either side, and huge wrap-around porches adorned each floor. A few lights were still on, illuminating the darkness.

Thaniel veered toward his left, and my mind raced. Where was he taking me? I had assumed we would stay in the castle. A garden came into view, surrounded by large weeping willow trees. To our left, a small cottage appeared.

"You don't live in the castle?"

He looked back at me. "I have my own quarters inside, but I prefer it out here. It's quieter."

He opened the front door, stepping back to allow me to pass. Before I could walk inside, something leaped at me. I shrieked, falling into Thaniel's arms. He caught me easily, setting me on my feet.

"Scraps, sit," he commanded.

The large brown dog sat on its hind legs, eyeing us eagerly. Thaniel stepped around me and the dog couldn't hold back anymore. It jumped on Thaniel, its front paws on his chest to leave him wet kisses.

"This is Scraps. She's very friendly."

I held my hand out, letting Scraps sniff me. She immediately wagged her tail. I bent, and she gave me a sloppy kiss.

"She likes you," Thaniel added.

I stood. "What breed is she, and what kind of name is Scraps?" I thought it was funny that his dog had such an odd name. For being the prince's pet, she should have a royal name.

"I'm not sure of her breed. She was found roaming the streets, looking for scraps of meat, actually anything to eat."

At hearing her name so frequently, Scraps sat, eyeing Thaniel expectantly. He moved inside, reappearing with a treat. Scraps gently removed it from his hand and disappeared inside the dark cottage.

"How old is she?"

He turned away, his eyes searching the darkness. "Six. I've had her since she was a puppy."

If what he was saying was true, that my family left this land five years ago, and I had been friends with him, I would have known Scraps. I searched my mind, prying for the smallest piece of memory, the tiniest seed of recognition, but found nothing.

Thaniel led me inside, turning on the lights. I blinked, letting my eyes adjust. His cottage was small and sparsely decorated. The only furniture in the living room was a couch, a wood stove, and a chair. There were no personal items, no knick-knacks, or pictures. Beyond the living room was a kitchen. To our right was another door, which I assumed was his bedroom.

"You can have the bed," he said, noticing my gaze lingering on the door. "I'll take the couch."

The thought of sleeping in the bed made my stomach churn. My parents and Addie were taken against their will. Why should I sleep in a comfortable bed? I should be looking for them. "When do you think we can leave?" I asked. "I'm anxious to find my parents and Addie. This isn't right. I don't even know if they're okay."

He crossed his arms over his chest. "We'll talk to my father tomorrow morning."

His response angered me. He hadn't even answered my question. I balled my fists, trying to calm my nerves. "We don't have a lot of time."

He nodded. "Once my father's retired for the night, no one's allowed to see him, myself included. I need his permission to reallocate some of our resources—soldiers, horses, scouts. Enley won't hurt them, not yet anyway. He's hoping to lure you to him. He wouldn't have had Addie answer when you called. We have a bit of time. I know it's not ideal—"

"No, it's not," I snapped.

He recoiled, and I took a moment to calm myself. He was only trying to help.

"I'm sorry. This isn't your fault."

"We'll figure it out," he agreed. "I think you need some sleep. It's been a long night." He stepped forward, toward his bedroom.

As much as I hated to agree with him, I was tired. I needed sleep.

His bedroom was just as sparse as the rest of the cottage. A large bed was against the wall and a plain wood dresser was to our right. He opened a drawer, removing an oversized shirt. "To sleep in. We'll have to get you some clean clothes tomorrow. There's a bathroom and a shower through there," he added, pointing to a door just beyond the bed. "If you need anything, let me know."

I nodded, too tired to say anything.

He left the room, closing the door behind him. I quickly made my way to the bathroom. I turned on the shower and let the room steam. I tossed my blood-stained dress on the floor and a weight lifted from my shoulders. It was cathartic, almost as if I were shedding the lies, stepping into the truth.

After my shower, I dressed in the oversized shirt. It was so large it fell just above my knees. I made my way to the bed and sat. I picked up my father's jacket and ran my fingers down the zipper. Another tear fell down my cheek. I couldn't stop the rest that followed. I cried for Addie; I cried for my parents. I even cried for George. I missed him and I wasn't sure why. He hadn't been the best boyfriend, and he had clearly moved on.

When my body couldn't handle any more tears, I fell into the bed. I closed my eyes and images of my parents appeared. I saw them as I had seen them last. They were on the front porch, waving as Addie pulled away. If I had known that would be the last time I'd see them, I would have said more. I would have told them I loved them. My stomach clenched, realizing the same could be said for Addie.

The last image that came to mind before I fell asleep was George. His arms around his date's waist, pulling her close. He lowered his head and brushed his lips on hers, breaking my heart all over again.

POPPY

NINE YEARS AGO

I was so hungry. With each rumble of my stomach, my insides burned. I hadn't eaten since my father came home with fresh-caught fish two nights ago. He had trapped them in the river. After paying his share to the king, it left us with two to split among three people.

My father hated the king. He hated the mandatory share he imposed on the kingdom. Every night my parents talked about moving on, finding another kingdom to move to. We had come to Marwood when I was one. We traded one tyrant king for another.

The Ashton-Dumont family was Shadow Marked. Large tattoos covered their bodies. I didn't quite understand, but knew it wasn't normal. My family wasn't marked.

I lay in a field of poppies, the soft breeze caressing me. The warm sun burned my cheeks, but I loved the field. Poppies were my mother's favorite flower. I was even named after them.

When my parents heard about the vast field, they stopped at Marwood. Eleven years later, we were still here. My parents often spoke of how hard it had been to move the first time, to pack up your life and set off for the unknown.

A long shadow crossed my vision, and I sat, searching for the source. Behind me, a boy walked toward the forest. He startled when he saw me.

"Hi," I called out.

The boy stopped walking. He was about my age, maybe a year or two older. His blond hair was cut short, and his clothes were freshly pressed. I looked down at my own well-worn dress, longing for something new. We hadn't had the money to buy new clothes this year.

He shifted on his feet. "I didn't see you there."

I smiled. "That's the point. I come here to relax, to hide from my parents."

The boy put his hands in his pockets. He looked toward the forest, then turned back to me. "Do you want to play?"

"Sure," I answered. "My name's Poppy. What's yours?"

The boy bit his lips, and his face scrunched, as if thinking. Finally, he said, "My name's not important."

I narrowed my eyes. What an odd answer. I stood from my field of poppies. "Well, what should I call you? Surely you have a name?"

A low whistle sounded. My heart rate increased. That was the sound of the army. They were on their way back to the castle from their month of training.

"Come on," I yelled excitedly. "That's the army. Maybe they'll have sweets for us!"

Without waiting for his answer, I skipped toward the city square. The boy shuffled behind me. Why wasn't he more excited? The soldiers were kind to us. They usually brought sweets from their travels. My mouth watered at the thought of the chocolate they had brought back last time.

When I reached the square, my stomach sank. It was packed. It seemed as if the entire kingdom had come to greet them. I ran toward the castle gate. It was relatively empty, everyone else was in the square. I was taking a chance; they may run out of treats before they reached me, but I was worried they wouldn't see me in the crowd. The boy stopped next to me.

"The last time they came through, I got a chocolate," I said. "Maybe they'll have more."

He nodded, looking around as if taking everything in for the first time. Where did he live? Perhaps he was the seamstress' nephew. The last time I had seen her, she mentioned her nephew would stay with her soon.

"Have you had chocolate before?"

The boy nodded again. He was silent. I would have to ask him about his family once the army passed.

By the time they made their way to us, I had given up any hope of treats. From the square, I heard laughter. My stomach coiled, angry that I missed out. A white horse passed us, and I looked up, meeting the gaze of the soldier atop. He waved, but continued on his way. Two more passed. My companion watched the army in mild interest.

"My last treat," a soldier called, looking at me and the boy. "I'm sorry, I only have one left."

I shifted on my feet. I really wanted it, but I had been the one to tell the boy about the procession. It would be wrong of me to take it.

"Give it to her," the boy said, surprising me. "I don't want it."

The soldier reached into his pocket. He withdrew a gold-foiled wrapper and tossed it to me. I caught it easily.

"They call that caramel," he said. "It's from a faraway land."

I studied the foiled wrapper in my hand, my excitement palpable. I had never heard of caramel before. I turned to the boy. "Are you sure you don't want it?"

His vivid blue eyes met mine. "I'm sure. I've had it before."

I hastily unwrapped the candy, wondering how wealthy my new friend was. He had caramel before I even heard about it. I placed the candy on my tongue, letting it melt in my mouth.

The boy stepped closer. "Do you like it?" When I nodded, he continued. "My name's Thaniel. It's nice to meet you, Poppy."

POPPY

My eyes snapped open. I was in Thaniel's bed, the room still dark. The dream had felt so real I could almost taste the caramel. Were these my memories coming back? I had met Thaniel in a field of poppies?

I closed my eyes again, willing the rest of the memory. All that met me was darkness. When nothing else came, I tried to go back to sleep but too many thoughts overtook me. When would we talk to the king? When would we leave? Where were my parents and Addie being held?

My muscles cramped, my anxious energy yearning for release. I flung my legs off the bed. When I opened the door, I was surprised to see the couch empty. The cottage was silent. I didn't even see Scraps. I walked to the front door, opening it slowly to peek outside.

Thaniel was sitting on the porch, his dog at his feet. He looked up when he heard me. "Did you sleep okay?"

How was I supposed to answer? Should I tell him about the memory? Was it even real, or only a dream? "Okay," I answered. "How about you?"

He shrugged. "Like normal. I don't sleep much, anyway."

The porch floor was cold on my bare feet. Faint rays of sunlight lit up the horizon, and I inhaled the crisp, cool air. I sat on an empty chair. Scraps looked up, saw that I didn't have any food, and immediately looked away. Apparently, I wasn't worth the effort this morning.

I ran my fingers through my hair, trying to detangle the knots. I looked at Thaniel, waiting for him to elaborate. Why didn't he sleep much? Did his people not need as much sleep? Was there something different in the air? Or the food they ate?

As silence overtook us, I opened my mouth, but the words didn't come. How was I going to tell him I may have remembered our first meeting?

"Did we meet in a field of poppies?"

He stilled. "We did."

"You gave me the caramel."

He smirked. "You looked so sad. I thought I was going to have to run inside the castle to bring you a chocolate."

While it was nice to have the validation that it had been more than a dream, a piece of the memory still tugged at me. "What were you doing outside of the castle that day? In the poppy field?"

Thaniel crossed his arms over his chest, looking out into the gardens. "I was going to the forest. To explore. I didn't have many friends, and Cerros didn't enjoy playing with me."

In the distance, a low whistle sounded. I sat straighter, my eyes darting through the gardens in front of us. Was something wrong?

"That's the changing of the guard," he said.

I relaxed into the chair again. "I'm surprised you were let out of the castle by yourself back then."

Thinking about it now, I'm surprised I had been by myself in the field of poppies. My parents were usually very protective. When I turned eighteen, they loosened their hold a bit.

"My brother's the heir," he answered. "My father was too concerned with Cerros and his education."

I let his answer settle. As an only child, I couldn't relate. I never had to compete with a sibling. I imagined the boy I had seen in the memory, vying for his family's attention, only to be rebuked because he wasn't the future king.

A younger woman appeared at the edge of the garden. A large garment bag was in her hands. Her long blonde hair shimmered in the sunlight and her wide-set blue eyes sparkled. Scraps looked up but didn't move.

"Who is that?" I asked. "Do you know her?"

Thaniel followed my gaze. He stood from his chair, making his way off the steps to join her. When they met, he wrapped his arms around her, giving her a quick hug. My stomach clenched, a tiny shard of jealousy flaring at their embrace.

What was wrong with me? I didn't care about Thaniel, not romantically. I needed him to help save my parents and Addie. After that, I would go home.

Thaniel turned back to me. "This is my sister, Theodora."

The woman stepped out of his embrace. "Thea. Everyone calls me Thea. Except Thaniel."

My stomach unraveled. I studied the woman as she made her way up the steps. She readjusted the bag in her hands when she was before me.

I stood. "Nice to meet you. I'm Poppy."

The woman smiled, revealing bright white teeth. She turned to Thaniel, almost as if she were confused. "You were actually telling the truth? I thought it was a joke."

I narrowed my eyes. What did that mean? All I had done was tell her my name. Then it hit me. Had I known her previously? Had I offended her?

"Poppy," Thaniel began as if searching for the right words, "you were actually friends with Thea as well."

I nodded, understanding her hesitation. She had been

expecting me to remember her. When I hadn't, it had been a shock. Even though five years had passed, she still had her memories.

I brought my arms to my chest. "I'm sorry. I don't remember any of this."

Thea brushed me off. "Thaniel already explained everything last night. I just assumed he was joking."

"You were here last night?"

She set the bag on Thaniel's chair and bent to pet Scraps. "I saw the lights were on. You were already asleep."

I awkwardly shifted on my feet. It was strange to be in the presence of not one, but two people I had a past with, and I couldn't even remember them. How close had we been?

I cleared my throat. "How did we meet?"

"We were friends first," Thaniel answered. "I introduced you. Thea liked to follow me. There were times I couldn't leave the castle without my shadow."

Thea rolled her eyes. "That's a bit of an exaggeration. You're my twin; I do like spending time with you."

My eyes darted from Thea back to Thaniel. They shared a resemblance; it shouldn't have come as a surprise that they were twins. Even their stance was the same. Their shoulders were pressed back, their posture rigid.

"When can we talk to the king?" I asked, pushing aside their banter.

"That's why I'm here." Thea picked up the garment bag. "I have clothes."

It was in that moment I realized I was only wearing Thaniel's oversized shirt. My cheeks burned. I ran my hands down the shirt, trying to pull it lower. Thea's eyes followed my movement, and she turned to her brother. I stepped inside, leaving them to their moment of unspoken communication. This wasn't the first impression I had been hoping for.

When Thea finally joined me, she pointed to her brother's

bedroom. When we were inside, she closed the door. She placed the garment bag on the bed and slowly opened it. She removed a short-sleeved cobalt-blue dress.

"This will work for breakfast. There's a pair of pajamas, another dress, and a few pants in here too."

I clasped my hands in front of me. "Thank you. I usually wear more than a shirt to bed."

Thea looked up. Our eyes met, and we laughed. A calmness fell over me as I relaxed into her warm presence. I studied the dress. While it was beautiful, was it really necessary? I was hoping we would leave this afternoon.

"You don't like it?" she asked, her head tilted to the side.

"It's beautiful. I just didn't know I would need to wear a dress. I'm hoping to leave soon. Once I have my family, I want to go back…to my home."

"You really don't remember him, do you?"

I shook my head. Even though one memory came back, Thaniel was still a stranger. The hair on my arms prickled, and I ran my palms over the skin, trying to warm myself.

She bit her lips. "You have to play the game. If you want my father to help, to release some of his soldiers, you need to play the part."

I sighed. I didn't quite understand. Play what part? Wouldn't he want to help? Wouldn't he want to do the right thing?

"My father's content," she added. "We've had no reliable threats in years. He won't want to start something with the Greys, especially since your parents left after the decree."

My stomach dropped. That wasn't the answer I had been hoping for.

"Here," she added, handing me the dress. "Try this on."

My legs trembled as I made my way to the bathroom. What was I going to do if the king wouldn't help? Would Thaniel be able to help me on his own? Could two people go against the

Greymoores? I didn't even know how many people we would be going up against.

After I dressed, I stepped back, looking at my reflection in the mirror. The face staring back at me wasn't my own. My skin was washed-out; my eyes lined in deep bags.

"Poppy?" Thea called. "Do you need help?"

I opened the door. "I don't suppose you have any makeup. I look exhausted."

She shook her head. "Makeup? Like rouge?"

"Forget it," I muttered.

"You look nice," she added. "Do you like it?"

I sighed. "It will have to do."

Thea looked away, studying her brother's room again. After an awkward moment of silence, she took a step forward, toward the door. I realized this was my chance to ask her a few questions, away from Thaniel.

"Are you Shadow Marked?" I asked, my eyes searching her body for any hidden marks.

She nodded. "Yes, although I haven't killed anyone. I don't plan on it either. But if I did...It effects everyone in our family."

When she answered, I remembered Thaniel had already mentioned his sister hadn't activated her curse. I couldn't seem to keep it all straight. There was too much being thrown at me.

"Is there really no way to stop it? The curse?"

She shrugged. "Not that we can figure."

I pulled my hair off my shoulders. I wished I had a hair tie. It had dried in big, frizzy waves and I wanted nothing more than to tie it back. I stepped closer, my next question on the tip of my tongue, aching to get out. "So, everything he's said is true?"

She crossed her arms over her chest. "What has he said? As you've seen, my brother does like to exaggerate."

"The fated part," I whispered. "He said that we're bonded, meant to be together. Is that really true?"

"Oh, that," she said casually, as if it were an ordinary thing.

"Yes, when his decree was announced, we were all shocked. I think Thaniel had been hoping it would be you, but it's not something that can be predicted."

"I don't feel any special bond with him," I said. "He seems nice enough. He saved my life. Twice now. If we were fated, wouldn't I feel something? Wouldn't I have a stronger connection?"

Her eyes darted across her brother's room, finally settling on me. "I imagine you will. Most of the fated do, even if they're not Shadow Marked. While our magmar could discern you as his fated, you won't necessarily feel the intensity of the bond that Thaniel feels. It's the same with my parents. My mother tried to fight it, but eventually the connection won."

"So, there's nothing I can do?" I asked, my heart rate spiking, imagining a life of forced marriage. I didn't even understand the whole fated concept or where it came from. How was I supposed to live with it?

Thea placed her hand on mine. "Thaniel won't force you to do something you don't want. That's the thing about my brother. He's honorable. He'll just make my life miserable."

I smiled at the joke. "Are you married? Has your decree been made?"

"No, neither I nor Cerros has found our fated. Perhaps one day soon we will." She moved to the door. "A word of advice. Don't tell my father you want to leave. If he thinks you'll stay with Thaniel, he may help."

I nodded. I could do that for my parents and Addie. I had to do something; I couldn't leave them. If that meant pretending to like Thaniel, I could play along.

She opened the door, leaving the bedroom. I took a deep breath, trying to steady my nerves. Rescuing my family may not be that easy after all.

POPPY

Thaniel's eyes were on me as I stepped out of the bedroom. He was standing near the front door. I hoped he hadn't heard my conversation with Thea. Scraps was now sitting on the couch, her head resting on a pillow.

"I'll see you later," Thea said, hugging Thaniel on the way out. "It's nice to see you again, Poppy."

I ran my hand along the smooth fabric of the dress. Before I could say goodbye, she had stepped outside, closing the door behind her in a flourish.

Thaniel's eyes met mine. "You look beautiful."

I wrapped my arms around my chest, trying to hide. I hated the attention. I didn't feel beautiful. I felt frantic, out of sorts.

Thaniel had changed since I last saw him. His blond hair was down, hanging loosely to his chin. He was wearing all black again.

"Black your favorite color?" I chided.

He bit his lip, holding back a laugh. "I want to show you something," he finally said, his voice deep. "Then we'll go to the castle."

Scraps was at his feet as I followed him out of the front door.

I was glad the dress was thin, as it had gotten very warm outside. I held my hand over my eyes, shading them from the bright sun.

Thaniel walked past the gardens, through the giant willow trees. I was grateful Thea had left comfortable shoes, but honestly, anything was better than the beat-up ballet flats. As we walked, I glanced around the grounds, looking for anything familiar, hoping that more memories would come. How long would it take for the rest? How had my parents even suppressed them? How had they given me new, fake ones? Thaniel had said it was magic, but I couldn't make sense of it.

As the large stone fence came into view, my mind raced. Where was he taking me? He waved to the guard stationed atop the post. As he climbed down, I noticed it wasn't Cullen. The guard opened the door to let us pass.

"We'll be back in a moment," Thaniel said.

The guard nodded.

Thaniel turned to the right, following the fence. A moment later, a field of flowers came into view. My hand flew to my chest. We were in the field of poppies. I ran ahead, surprised that the field looked exactly as it had in my dream, how I remembered it five years ago. The field of red and white flowers took my breath away. Scraps ran ahead, chasing a large blue butterfly.

"This is where we met," Thaniel said. "It's only fitting I bring you here first, since you remembered it."

I closed my eyes and held my arms wide, the warm sunshine bathing me. I spun in a circle, taking it all in. I finally felt at peace, as if I were home. The field of wild poppies invigorated me.

"You like it?" he asked, his voice pulling me back.

I opened my eyes. He had been watching me. A slight smile lit up his face, as if he were enjoying my amusement.

"It's exactly as I remember. Every blade, every petal."

He put his hands in his pockets. "I come here a lot. It reminds me of you."

I spun around again, taking in every detail, thinking of the best way to answer. I didn't want to lead him on, give him false hope for a relationship I wasn't even ready to begin. My baggage was more than he could carry.

It felt as if I were repeating myself, but it had to be said. "You know I'm going back to White Bridge."

He looked at his feet. "I won't stop you. Will you go back to George?"

I shrugged, answering the only way I could, "I don't know."

He looked away. "I imagined what it would be like when you finally came home…when you learned about the decree. You would have been happy. I thought this would be easier."

"That's not fair," I said. "You have all our memories. I don't."

"I wish I could forget them." His eyes met mine. "If you don't remember, I don't want to."

I placed my fingers on the bridge of my nose, trying to think clearly. "I don't know what to say. The truth is, you're still a stranger to me."

Thaniel jerked his head up. "The truth? I burned these poppies to the ground three years ago. Every last one. They come back year after year, just as strong and vibrant as ever. I'll always love you, Poppy. Even as you forget me, even as you move on with your life, I'll be here, staring into this field. I tried to forget you. I tried to let you move on, but the mere thought of you haunted me."

My breath stilled, and the hair on my arms stood, his words sending shivers down my spine. I opened my mouth, searching for the air I desperately needed but couldn't seem to find. Thaniel looked away. I wanted to run to him, but something held me back.

"I don't want to keep you any longer than necessary," he finally said. "My father is expecting us."

I didn't move, as if the poppies were rooting me to the field. I wanted to yell at him; I wanted to scream that it wasn't fair he was putting these expectations on me. Instead, I closed my eyes and pictured my parents. I took a deep breath and stepped forward, finally breaking free.

THANIEL

I hadn't been exaggerating when I told Poppy I burned the field three years ago. I was tired of looking at them, a constant reminder of my loss. As the flames spread, I thought it would release me. When only ash remained, I realized the curse was stronger. I could never forget her.

A part of me thought Poppy would remember everything when I brought her to our field. It was the place we met. It was the first memory that pushed its way forward. I hated to admit it, but just as I was a stranger to her, she was a stranger to me. Five years had changed us both.

Morgan was waiting for us when we reached the guard tower. He opened the door, bowing as I passed. An icy chill washed over me. I hated when anyone bowed to me. Even though it was all I knew, it felt wrong. I would never be king, as my father liked to remind me every chance he got.

I would also never have Poppy. She had already made it very clear that she was going to go back to White Bridge with her family…and George. My stomach clenched at the thought of her ex-boyfriend.

By the time I had found her two years ago, she had already

been dating George. There was nothing I could do except hope she was happy. Cerros liked to joke that I could take her, even against her will, force the memories back, but even he wasn't that cruel.

In the courtyard, a warm breeze rustled the blades of grass that had yet to be cut. I balled my hands into fists, digging my nails into the flesh. How were we going to get through breakfast? How was I going to ask my father for help when her parents willingly left, taking her with them after the decree?

He would never agree, especially if Poppy didn't even want to stay in Marwood. He would see right through us. It would be up to me to rescue her parents.

If they had only stayed, they wouldn't even need rescuing. The irony.

Beside me, Poppy exhaled slightly, the sound catching my attention. Her eyes darted through the courtyard, taking it all in. In that moment, I knew I would do whatever it took to rescue her parents, to see the weight lifted from her shoulders. Even if she didn't love me, I loved her. I would do anything to make her happy, even if that meant letting her go.

Although the morning wasn't going as planned, I was determined to put on a good front and convince the king to help. When we arrived back in the gardens, I walked in step with Thaniel, working up the courage to talk to him. We needed to act as a united front. We needed to act in love.

Thaniel kept his gaze steady. He didn't look at me once. I was angry, scared, and confused, and he wasn't helping the situation. For being his fated, he was acting incredibly selfish.

"Can we talk?" I asked. "We need a plan. Thea told me it would be best to pretend we were in love."

I paused. He had told me he loved me in the poppy field. He said he would always love me. A pit formed in my belly. How had my life spiraled so out of control?

He stopped walking. "That's something I don't have to pretend."

"I know," I said in a rush. "I didn't mean to bring it up again."

"She's right," he said. "Just pretend I'm George. Act like you want to spend the rest of your life with me. If he thinks you're open to the decree, he'll be easier to convince."

"I don't even know if I want to be with George," I whispered. "Just give me time to process everything."

He pressed his lips together but didn't answer. A silence descended upon us, and I let it fall. It wasn't my fault that I couldn't remember anything. I had memories that weren't even real. The last five years had been a lie, and I was still coming to terms with it.

I took a moment to gather my thoughts. The castle was even bigger than it had appeared last night. By day, it was imposing. The white stone sparkled in the sunlight, the turrets too many to count. My legs trembled as I traversed the steep stone steps, bypassing the guards stationed at the doors. I recognized Cullen, the soldier we had met last night.

Thaniel leaned close, his whisper sending chills down my spine. "After breakfast, we'll get an audience with my father."

I hadn't been expecting to wait, but figured now wasn't the time to complain. I needed the king to feel sorry for me. I needed him to want to help.

Thaniel led me into the foyer, and my breath caught in my throat. The room was luxurious. A large crystal chandelier reflected the sunlight onto the white marble floor. Large windows lined the wall, and a massive double staircase was before us. A strong floral scent curled around me. In between the double staircase, a glossy black shelf held an assortment of white flowers, their leaves lined with thin pink lines.

Thaniel bent his arm, inviting me to take it. The room was silent as I looped my arm through his. He led me up the stairs slowly.

"I'm sorry," he said. "I know I'm not being fair. This is hard for me, but I know it's harder for you."

I nodded, my nerves making it hard to think clearly. When we reached the top of the staircase, we turned right. We made our way down the long hall. The sound of laughter met my ears, and I stiffened, nervous about what was to come.

Before us, a large doorway beckoned. Thaniel squeezed my arm and led me into a large dining hall.

"There he is," a voice called. "And his fated."

Thaniel stopped. He bowed his head low, gesturing for me to do the same. I followed suit, the blood rushing to my head, making me dizzy.

"Come sit," the voice said. "You're just in time."

Thaniel pulled out a chair, inviting me to take it. I looked up, meeting the hard gaze of a woman in front of me. Her long blonde hair was braided down her back. She had the reddest lips I had ever seen. Next to the woman was an older man wearing a gold crown. His white tunic was spotless. He smiled when our eyes met.

Next to me, Thaniel cleared his throat. "Poppy, these are my parents."

"It's nice to meet you," my voice cracked.

"We're glad you're home," the king said, glancing from me to Thaniel and back again. "I know the past five years have taken a toll on my son."

"We're taking things slow," Thaniel said, fiddling with the napkin at his setting. "There's no need to rush...now that we found each other."

The king's smile fell. "Is everything okay?"

Thaniel nodded. I placed my arms on the table before realizing it may not be proper. No one else had their arms resting at their place setting. Thaniel reached for my hand and squeezed it, stroking my thumb. His touch sent another shiver down my spine.

"I remember how hard it was," the king continued, picking up the glass in front of him. He took a big gulp before continuing, "When I was waiting for your mother, it was the worst pain of my life. I couldn't eat, I couldn't sleep."

Thaniel turned away, and I remembered his comment from earlier. Had he not been sleeping because of our bond? Maybe he didn't have it any easier. He couldn't control who he was fated to. Thea had said that he would never force me, but what would that mean if I went home and settled with George, or someone else? Would he never move on? Would he always be in love with me? The girl he could never have.

"Thaniel, is everything okay?" the queen asked. "You don't seem happy."

Beside me, he stiffened. His hands fell to his lap.

"It's my fault," I said. "We were up really late, I—"

"Oh, no need to explain," the king said. "I remember those first few nights. We have a wedding to plan."

My mouth ran dry. My jaw slackened, trying to comprehend what he'd said. Wedding? I couldn't marry Thaniel.

"We don't want to rush things," Thaniel added. "We'd actually like to speak with you about something."

"I'm so sorry we're late." Thea waltzed into the room with a man by her side. "I hope we didn't miss anything."

Thaniel looked at me, our gaze lingering too long. My cheeks flushed, and I reached for my glass. I let the liquid wash down my throat, carrying away my nerves.

"You're just in time," the queen said.

I looked at Thaniel again, wondering if he was always brushed aside. My gaze fell on Thea and the man she had entered with. He looked familiar, and it only took a moment to recognize him. It was Thaniel's brother, Cerros. I turned away, wondering what he did with the woman's body.

Two servers appeared, placing tall, gold flutes in front of each setting. When they left, the king held his up in a toast. Everyone at the table picked up theirs as well, so I followed suit.

"To Thaniel and Poppy."

The king brought his glass to his lips, inhaling the liquid inside. Next to me, Thea's spilled, her bubbly drink spreading across the table. I quickly set my flute down and reached for my napkin. I wiped at the liquid coming my way.

"What happened?" Cerros asked.

"You're always so clumsy, Thea," Thaniel chided.

Thea blotted the table with her napkin. "I didn't mean to. I was really looking forward to that."

"Here, have mine," I said. "I'm going to stick with water."

I didn't know what the liquid was, and I needed to stay sharp. Hopefully, Thaniel and I would have time to talk to the king later. I passed the flute to Thea.

"Are you sure?"

I nodded. "Have at it."

Thea brought it to her lips. I reached for my water and took a long sip. Before I had a chance to set my glass back on the table, Thea slumped forward, the flute shattering. Thaniel and Cerros rushed from their chairs, dashing to their sister.

"The drink," Cerros said, his face paled.

Thaniel stuck his fingers in the puddle at his sister's feet, bringing them to his nose. "Claredium."

The king stood from his chair, and pandemonium broke out. Servers rushed into the room, stopping at Thea's still body. My mind turned over the past few minutes. What was claredium? Poison?

Thaniel turned to me. "That was meant for you."

Thaniel picked up his sister, cradling her in his lap. He looked up, his gaze stopping on me. The room spun, and a low, muffled ring echoed in my ears.

Someone had tried to poison me. Thaniel said I would be safe here. A hand fell on my shoulder.

Cullen's eyes swept over me. "Are you okay?"

I didn't know how to answer. Should I give the family privacy? I didn't know if Thea was even alive. It felt as if I was in everyone's way. The room was now crowded, crammed with soldiers and staff all trying to help.

"I should wait outside. I'm in the way."

"No," Thaniel growled. "You stay here, with me."

I didn't protest. In a way, it was safer in the busy room. What good would it do to step into the hall, an easy target to finish?

Thaniel turned to another soldier. "Take Thea to her room."

The soldier knelt, lifting the princess in his arms. Her head rolled back, and my hand flew to my mouth.

I turned to Cullen. "Is she…"

"No," he answered, his lips pressed into a thin line. "She'll pull through."

Thaniel was before me in an instant. He took my arm and pulled me close, his grip too tight. I tried pulling back, but he wouldn't loosen his hold.

"You're hurting me."

He looked down, and I saw the tears in his eyes. "I won't let anything happen to you."

"Just loosen your grip a little," I said. "I'm right here. I'm not going anywhere."

He looked away, but loosened his grip.

We watched the soldier carry Thea out of the dining hall. As the room cleared, Thaniel stepped toward the door, bringing me with him. We walked down the long hall in the opposite direction of the entrance.

So many questions floated through me. Who would want to poison me? Would Thea be okay? Would we still have time to speak with the king? This last question sent a ripple of guilt coursing through me. I was sorry for Thaniel, but I needed my own family back.

When we reached the end of the long hallway, he led me up a dimly lit set of stairs. "Stay close."

I didn't answer. Where did he think I was going to go? I didn't know the castle. I knew the safest place was by his side. As frustrating as he was, he wouldn't hurt me. He had plenty of chances already.

My heart hammered in my chest as my eyes adjusted to the lack of light. We walked in silence, my fear and confusion clouding me. When he pointed to a large glossy black door, I exhaled, relieved we would be safe. He stepped in front of me and reached into his pocket. He withdrew a silver key and inserted it into the lock. With one last glance down the hall, he pushed it open, ushering me inside. Before turning on the lights, he locked the door again.

"Where are we?" I whispered.

"My quarters."

Bright light filled the room. We were standing in the biggest bedroom I had ever seen. A large bed was opposite us, in front of tall floor-to-ceiling windows. The curtains were a plush red velvet. Two dressers and a couch were to our right, before a stone fireplace. A thick rug covered the stone floor.

Thaniel walked in front of me, searching for any threats. I watched him, rooted to the floor, trying to take everything in. What exactly did his quarters mean? Was this his room?

An uncomfortable silence descended upon us. I wrapped my arms around my chest, my fingers running along the satiny fabric of my dress.

"Have a seat," he said, finally noticing I hadn't moved. "Make yourself comfortable."

He disappeared through a doorway I hadn't seen. When he reappeared, he sat on the bed. He placed his head in his hands. His back shook slightly. Was he crying? It didn't seem right. He was larger than life, a force all his own. His breathing stilled, and I debated what to do. Should I comfort him? Leave him alone?

I sat next to him. I took his hand, squeezing it gently, letting him know he wasn't alone. When he looked up, his eyes were red, lined with tears.

"Will she be okay?" I asked.

He nodded. "If it had been you..."

I didn't know how to take that. Why would it have been any different? "What was in the drink?"

His eyes swept the room. "Claredium. It's derived from the root of a fairly common plant. It's deadly in large doses."

I stiffened. "But she'll be all right?"

"My father's paranoid," he answered. "We've been drinking claredium tea since we were young. We started with small doses and have worked our way up. In small quantities, we can tolerate it." His eyes met mine. "You wouldn't have. Thea will be out of it for the next few days, but she'll get the care she needs."

My body trembled. How had this even happened? My mind replayed the moment the servers brought in our drinks. Everything seemed fine.

"We used to tease him about his paranoia..." the statement tapered off.

We sat in silence. I still couldn't wrap my head around everything that had happened in the last 24 hours. Nothing made sense anymore.

"Who would want to poison me?"

"Enley," he answered, his breathing hard. "I'll kill him myself. I just don't know how he came so close. How he got to us in our home."

I looked away, my thoughts too much to bear. Maybe Enley had already killed my parents and Addie. My stomach sank. I needed to find them.

"As soon as Thea's better, we'll talk to my father."

"I don't have time," I said. "There's nothing keeping him from killing my family. He's not luring me; he's trying to kill me from afar."

Thaniel wiped the tears from underneath his eyes. "Tonight. We'll talk to him tonight."

I sighed; a weight lifted from me. If all went well, we would be on our way tonight. Then I could go back to White Bridge and hopefully live a normal life once more.

POPPY

FIVE YEARS AGO

The rain had dampened my spirits. I had been looking forward to playing in the poppy field with Thaniel. It was my birthday, and he had told me we could do anything I wanted. I had been looking forward to lounging in the field of flowers.

I backed up against the enormous tree trunk, trying to keep my new dress dry. I ran a hand down the emerald fabric. It was the nicest dress I had ever owned. My parents had given it to me for my birthday. My father had been very successful this year, and we were finally able to enjoy some of the profit. His wood-working skills were finally being recognized.

When the rough bark snagged the lace, I stepped forward. I was gently untangling the fabric when I heard someone behind me. I spun around to find Thaniel. His bright blue eyes ran down me and I stilled. The rain intensified, and he moved closer, seeking refuge under the tree limbs.

He reached into his pocket, withdrawing a thin rectangle box wrapped in a blue bow. "You look lovely."

"Thank you," I answered, smiling at the present.

"How old are you now, ten?" he teased.

I narrowed my eyes, not pleased with the joke. "Sixteen."

"Well, are you going to open it?" he asked. "Or shall we watch the rain a bit longer?"

I shook the box slightly, trying to guess what delights it held. Every year, he brought me the same present. He had the king's personal baker make me the sweetest chocolate treats. They were the most decadent sweets I had ever eaten. His presents were always my favorite. I couldn't imagine growing up with them so readily available. How lucky he was to be a prince!

I carefully lifted the lid on the box. A surprised gasp escaped my lips. Nestled inside were large caramel candies. The same candies the soldier had given me the first day I had met Thaniel.

"I know it's not chocolate," his voice cracked. "But meeting you was one of the best days of my life. Every time I see the caramels, I think of you. I thought you would like them."

My heart thrummed so fast I feared I may pass out. I quickly covered the caramels, hoping that if I dropped the box, they would at least be safe from the mud and grass. Meeting Thaniel had been one of the best days of my life. I truly valued our friendship. Even though we were so different, and had practically nothing in common, I enjoyed our time together. Hearing that he felt the same way was the best birthday gift I could have asked for.

"I love them," I said. "Thank you."

He looked away. A low rumble of thunder echoed around us.

"Isn't Princess Lara coming today?" I asked. "Maybe she'll be your fated."

Even as I said the words, I wished I hadn't. I hated that one day someone was going to take him from me. We would no longer be friends. He would marry a noblewoman, probably a princess. I would be lucky to find a tradesman. I didn't hold on to the romanticized notion I would marry for love. I knew I would marry out of necessity. There would be no more chocolate, or caramels, in my future.

"She is," he answered, still watching the rain. "I don't think she's my fated."

I gripped the box tighter. "Why not?"

"It's only a feeling. Maybe I don't have a fated. Gabriel doesn't. He's still single, happy as can be."

I looked away, thinking of the king's advisor. Gabriel was still young; in his twenties. He could still have a fated. A small part of me hoped Thaniel wouldn't. Maybe we could continue our friendship after all. As soon as the thought came, I dismissed it. Our friendship would eventually have to end. I would need to marry, and I couldn't marry a prince.

I sighed. "Don't say that. You'll find your happily ever after."

"What about you?" He turned to me; our eyes locked. "Will you get yours?"

His question echoed in my head. Would I get my happily ever after? Probably not. A part of me hoped I would, but the realistic part of me knew I may not. I only hoped that the man I married would be kind.

Thaniel stepped closer. "Maybe we can marry. There's no one else I want to be with. We could be happy."

My breath fluttered. For a moment, I let the words sink, imagining it could actually be possible. I would be happy with Thaniel. Even if he wasn't a prince, even if he was a normal tradesman. Like the thunder that cracked around us, the thought shattered.

"You know that can't happen," I said. "I'm only the carpenter's daughter."

He gripped my arms, pulling me close. "We can run away together."

My eyes met his again, and my body stilled. Every part of me was screaming yes. I wanted to run away with him. I wanted to be with him. But we were so young.

Thaniel placed his hands on either side of my head, leaning close. His lips met mine. I dropped the box of caramels but didn't care. I wrapped my arms around his neck, pulling him even closer.

Suddenly, another boom of thunder echoed around us, so close I feared it had hit the tree. I jumped out of his arms and my hands flew to my chest. As if on cue, we both began laughing.

The sound of horses brought us back. A large white carriage passed by the castle gate. My stomach dropped. Maybe Princess Lara would be his fated. Maybe all I would have to remember him by was our stolen kiss and a box of caramels. I bent, retrieving them. Thankfully, they hadn't gotten wet.

"I think you're my fated," he whispered. "I can't imagine my life with anyone but you."

My cheeks flushed. "The magmar would have made your decree by now."

He shook his head. "Maybe she's losing the ability. Maybe she just hasn't seen it yet."

I took his hands, squeezing them. "We're from two very different worlds. We'll both find our happy endings."

He nodded slowly. "I'll meet you tomorrow?"

"Only if you bring me some chocolate," I answered. "They'll go great with my caramels."

His eyes lit up. "My father has these cherry chocolates; I think you'll like them."

His eyes met mine one last time before he stepped into the rain. I watched him disappear into the storm, somehow knowing it would be the last time I would see him.

POPPY

When I opened my eyes, I was surprised to find I was lying on Thaniel's chest. He was still asleep, his lips curved into a slight smile. Faint light leaked through the windows, trying to push its way past the dark storm clouds. My mouth was dry, tainted from sleep.

Thaniel stirred. When he didn't wake, I gently rolled over, extracting myself from his grip. I didn't remember falling asleep, especially in his arms. The events of the last day must have taken a lot out of me. I ran the palms of my hands down my arms, rubbing away the tiny goosebumps.

The memory of my sixteenth birthday flooded me. According to Thaniel, my family and I had left when I was sixteen. We must have left shortly after my birthday. A shiver ran through me when I remembered our stolen kiss.

Thaniel mumbled in his sleep, "No, no, no, no." Sweat pooled at his brow and his body twitched.

I placed my hand on his arm, gently shaking him. "Wake up."

His eyes flashed open. "How long have I been asleep?"

"I don't know," I answered. "I just woke up. Were you having a nightmare?"

"I always do." He turned toward the window.

I watched the rain slide down the glass in long, thin strips. Our kiss replayed in my mind, over and over. I wanted to tell him what I remembered, but the silence was too heavy.

Finally, he stood. "We should get ready."

I slid toward the edge of the mattress when a knock sounded. He turned to me, our eyes meeting for only a moment. Another sharp tap on the door broke his gaze from mine. He placed his hand on his hip, underneath his shirt, and I saw the glint of silver. His knife.

"Thaniel," a voice called. "It's me."

He unlocked the door, pulling it open.

Cerros stepped into the room, quickly closing the door behind him. "Thea's awake."

Thaniel stepped forward. "I want to see her."

Cerros shook his head. "You know you can't."

"I'm her twin," Thaniel said. "She'll want to see me."

"It doesn't matter," Cerros answered. "I'm her brother too, and the future king, and I can't even see her."

I didn't want to interrupt their conversation and felt awkward sitting on the bed. I bit my lips, turning to face the window again.

"Dinner will be served shortly," Cerros said. "Father had his private chef prepare everything. No one was allowed in the kitchen."

Thaniel sighed. "We need to talk to him anyway. We're going to ask him to help, to spare a few soldiers to look for Poppy's family."

I turned back to them. Now that the conversation had shifted, it only felt right that I could be a part of it.

Cerros crossed his arms over his chest. "I'm not sure how that's going to go over."

"I'll go by myself if I have to," Thaniel said. "Her family's been kidnapped because of our bond. It's not right."

Cerros stepped forward. "I know. If I have to, I'll go with you. You're not going by yourself."

I cleared my throat. "Actually, he won't be going by himself."

Cerros turned to face me, the confusion evident.

"I'm going," I added.

He snapped back to Thaniel. "You're allowing this?"

"It's what she wants," Thaniel said.

Cerros shook his head, as if he couldn't believe his brother's answer. "If that's what you think is for the best."

"It is," Thaniel said. "I'll never take away her free will. She can make her own decisions."

I watched their exchange silently, wondering if I should interject, when a question sprung into my head. Why had Cerros been in White Bridge? I understood Thaniel's reasons… sort of, but it just seemed out of place that the future king would be there too. Then something else came to mind.

How had the woman found me? How had Enley found me?

Thaniel and Cerros were still talking, but my mind was reeling.

"Why were you in White Bridge?" I asked.

Thaniel pinched the bridge of his nose. "We already went over this."

"Not you," I said. I turned to Cerros. "Why were you there?"

"Thaniel has a house there," he answered. "I was staying with him."

I turned to Thaniel. "You have a house there?"

He rubbed his forehead. "I was going to tell you."

Even though I wanted to press him, to find out why he had a house in White Bridge, I trudged on. I didn't want to lose my train of thought. Something bigger was at play, and I was determined to figure it out. "How did that woman find me? How did Enley know where I live?"

Thaniel and Cerros exchanged a look. I waved my hand, waiting for them to share their thoughts.

"I've been wondering the same," Thaniel finally answered. "I don't know how he was able to find you."

I let that settle, turning it over in my head. The fact that I was almost poisoned—that Thea was—inside of the castle made me think there was a spy, someone on the inside working for Enley.

My gaze met Thaniel's, and I knew he was thinking the same.

THANIEL

*P*oppy was on to something. Cerros and I had our suspicions. It was reassuring to hear that she had the same, that we weren't being paranoid.

Word had spread among the Greys that Enley had found my fated. I hadn't believed the rumors at first. How could he have found her? While it had been relatively easy for me, because of our connection, it didn't make sense that Enley would have the same luck.

Poppy crossed her arms over her chest. "I still want to know about your house in White Bridge."

While I had ulterior motives, it was a smart business move. Our family still had connections in the land Poppy now called home. When my grandfather claimed the throne for himself, he realized he could expand his newfound wealth in trade. Marwood was rich with diamonds and rubies. While we didn't have contacts in White Bridge specifically, it hadn't been hard to convince my father it was a good opportunity.

"I'll take you there whenever you want," I said.

"It's small," Cerros added. "I don't think you'll like it."

Poppy relaxed her stance. "Do you think Enley has someone on the inside? Someone working in the castle?"

I nodded. As much as I hated to admit it, it was the only thing that made sense. Someone had been following me. Someone had almost killed my fated. If she had drunk the wine…I would have lost her before she had a chance to remember.

"They won't be around much longer," Cerros said. "I'm already on it."

I balled my hands into fists. "Now that Thea's been poisoned, father will be on it too."

My forehead ached, and I ran a hand above my eyebrows, trying to ease the pressure. My nap had been too short. Honestly, I was surprised I had fallen asleep at all. As much as I craved it—the release from my thoughts, pressures, expectations—it eluded me. Even when I could fall asleep, I was usually plagued with nightmares, like the one I had just awoken from.

Sweat pooled at the base of my neck. It was a dream I couldn't shake, a memory I couldn't forget. I hadn't even met Princess Lara, but I was sure the magmar was going to announce her name.

My knees buckled as I walked up the stairs, the ivory columns leading the way. I couldn't believe the magmar had called for me, that she had sensed my fated moments after I confessed my love for Poppy. The Universe could be harsh, that much I knew, I just hadn't realized how harsh.

When the magmar spoke Poppy's name, I thought I had been dreaming. I couldn't move, too afraid to break the moment. By the time I fully comprehended that everything I had ever wanted was finally coming true, that I could be with Poppy, word had spread.

I knew her father was in the castle. A few months ago, my mother wanted a new barn constructed. Our usual carpenter was already occupied. I had told my father about Flinn Mathews, a local carpenter I had met, and he agreed to hire him.

I knew Poppy's family was struggling. I had only been trying to help. Now his services were highly sought after among the nobility, which meant he would hear about the decree any moment. I had to be the one to tell Poppy.

I ran out the door, past those eagerly watching the display. I never fully understood the appeal of a decree. I couldn't wrap my head around the fact that people were interested in hearing who others were fated to.

The rain was cold on my skin. My lungs burned as I placed one foot in front of the other. My calves ached, but I couldn't wait to tell Poppy that one day we could be together, that she didn't have to worry about marrying someone she didn't love. We would finish our studies. Now that she was my fated, she could study at the castle with me.

I darted up the front steps. Underneath the porch awning, I took a moment to catch my breath. I straightened my shirt before reaching out and knocking. My heart beat in time with the rain as I waited. When no one answered, I raised my hand to knock again and saw the door wasn't latched all the way.

My fingers curled around the doorknob. I pushed it open. "Poppy? Are you here?"

Silence met me.

I took another step forward as a boom of thunder echoed, sending chills down my spine. The hair on my arms prickled when a flash of lightning lit up the dark sky, illuminating the house. It looked as if everything of value had been taken.

My stomach sank when I found Poppy's room in the same disarray. My boot pushed something into the floor as I stepped forward. I knelt, my hands finding the box of caramels. I ran my finger along the ribbon. Poppy wouldn't have left them behind. I fell to my knees. The Universe dangled the possibility of happiness for only a moment.

"What do we do now?" Poppy's voice cut through the memory.

I looked up. "We talk to my father."

POPPY

I followed Thaniel and Cerros down the hall. My eyes swept through the dark, searching for threats. I didn't feel safe in the castle. I didn't think I would ever feel safe again until I was home. A sinking feeling washed over me. Would I even be safe there?

The sound of our feet echoed through the stone halls. We had already passed through Thaniel's wing of the castle. I still didn't understand why he needed an entire wing of rooms for his use, along with the cottage. It seemed excessive. I glanced at Cerros, wondering if his quarters were grander as the future king.

Flashes of my dream haunted me, pulling me closer to Thaniel. The way our lips touched, the soft pressure of his arms around me, made the hair on the back of my neck prickle. Had I even heard the decree? Had I known we were fated before my parents brought me to White Bridge? Before they erased my memories.

The betrayal stung. I knew I would forgive them. In time. They had their reasons, the biggest being that Thaniel, and his entire family, were Shadow Marked. Just seeing the marks on his chest was a lot to take in. But they didn't know Thaniel, not like I had. From my memories, I saw something in him that was more than his curse.

"Poppy?" Thaniel asked, his brow furrowed. "Are you okay?"

I looked up. "I'm fine. Lost in thought."

He nodded. "We're almost there. Remember—"

I waved him off. "Don't eat or drink anything off my plate. I know, I know."

Thaniel had already gone over this. Our plan was to share the food on his plate. He pressed his lips together, clearly unhappy with my nonchalance. I had to admit; I wasn't happy either. I didn't know where it came from, but it wasn't like me.

"Everything will be fine," Cerros said. "Right now, the only one with access to our food and drink is father's personal chef."

"I don't trust anyone," Thaniel muttered under his breath.

We stopped at a large door outlined in gold. Small engravings were carved on the wood. I tried to make out what they were, but Thaniel pushed the door open too quickly. Bright light filled my vision, a stark contrast to the dark hallway. I narrowed my eyes, letting them adjust when the king spoke, "I've been told Thea is much better."

A wave of guilt washed over me. A part of me felt responsible for her poisoning, as if I had done it myself. I knew it was ridiculous. I had done nothing wrong, but I couldn't shake the feeling.

Thaniel led me to the large table. We were in the king's private chambers. If Thaniel's room was large, I didn't know what to classify this as. It was the biggest, grandest room I had ever been in. There wasn't even enough furniture to fill the massive space. Large floor-to-ceiling windows were to my right. A crystal chandelier was above the table, the light casting multi-colored sparkles around the room. Paintings in gold frames lined the walls. At the opposite end, a large sitting room beckoned.

As everyone settled, I reached for the glass of water in front of me. Thaniel placed his hand on mine, and I stopped. How had I already forgotten our plan? I moved my arm from underneath his and placed it on my lap.

"How are you feeling, Poppy?"

I looked up. The king was watching me, his hands steepled in front of him. I sucked in a large lungful of air before answering, "As good as can be expected."

"Stay with Thaniel. He'll protect you."

Thaniel cleared his throat. "Something has to be done."

The king turned to his son. "What else would you have me do?"

"I was hoping to speak with you later," Thaniel began. "Enley was in White Bridge. If I hadn't been watching her…"

I bit my lip, thinking of what would have happened if Thaniel hadn't been at McLaughlin's. That woman would have killed me. The only silver lining in that reality was the possibility that Enley wouldn't have taken my parents and Addie. At least they would be safe.

Cerros cleared his throat. "He has Poppy's parents."

"And my best friend, Addie," I added.

"We need to do something," Thaniel said. "Poppy's not even safe here. No one is. Someone's working with him. There's no other explanation for how he could have found her."

The king leaned back in his chair. "Tell me what happened. From the beginning."

Thaniel told his father everything that had happened. I listened, only interjecting once to explain the layout of my house when the king asked. The queen sat in silence; her brow furrowed the entire time.

When Thaniel finished, he leaned forward, looking at his father. "We need a few soldiers."

"They stay here. If there's another attack—"

"There won't be," Thaniel interrupted. "Poppy and I are leaving. With or without your help."

My heart hammered in my chest. Everyone's eyes were on me. From the silence, I could tell the king and queen hadn't been expecting it. Thaniel placed his arm on mine again, drawing me away from my thoughts.

The king turned to me. "You're going?" When I nodded, he looked at Thaniel. "Is that wise?"

"All I want is for her to be happy."

"But for her to go—"

"I will not stop her," Thaniel said, his voice calm.

I bit my tongue to keep from interjecting. It wasn't my discussion. This was for Thaniel and his father. I was going to find my parents with or without the king's help.

"Why are you so eager to find them?" the queen asked. "They took her from you. They never gave you a chance."

I looked at Thaniel, hoping he wouldn't take the bait. He sighed but didn't meet my gaze. My hands shook as I suppressed the urge to answer, to defend my parents.

At the silence, the queen continued, "Think of the years of pain they've caused this family. Surely this is for the best. They're no longer stopping you from being together."

My hands trembled. Had I heard her correctly? Was she insinuating that my parents deserved this? My forehead throbbed.

"They had their reasons," I said. "My parents were only protecting me."

"You don't have to say anything, Poppy," Thaniel said.

It took everything inside of me to keep quiet. I didn't want to make the situation worse. I didn't want to give them another reason to withhold aid.

The queen placed her napkin on her lap. "If that's what you want."

"We don't have many we can spare at the moment," the king

added. "I suppose you already have a plan? When are you leaving?"

I turned to Thaniel, eagerly waiting for his answer. My mouth ran dry.

"Tomorrow morning."

"So soon," the king mumbled. "I suppose I can send Lucien. He can ride ahead and scout for any danger. You'll have to set a rendezvous point."

Thaniel looked at his brother. "The old inn. In Denreas."

The king nodded. "Cerros?"

I turned to Thaniel's brother, waiting to see where the conversation was heading. Cerros looked up.

"I take it you'll ride out with your brother?" the king asked.

Cerros nodded. "Yes."

"Is that necessary?" the queen asked. "You're the heir."

He didn't miss a beat. "Poppy is my brother's fated. Nothing we say will convince him to stay. I want to ensure he comes back. We all know I'm the better fighter."

Next to me, Thaniel snorted. "If you say so."

"I'll see what I can do," the king said. "Now let's eat."

The chef stepped forward. He set a plate in front of the king. As the rest of our food was brought out, I relaxed, the tension leaving my body. I had a feeling things were turning around. We would find my parents and I could finally go home.

I turned to Thaniel, giving him a big smile. I almost missed the look of concern he shared with Cerros. My stomach sank. Maybe he wasn't so confident in our plan after all.

Thaniel narrowed his eyes at me, not pleased with my answer. He had asked if I remembered seeing anyone suspicious in White Bridge the last few days. He was still trying to figure out who was working with Enley and how he had found my family so easily. "The only suspicious person I had seen was you," rolled off my lips before I could stop it.

"Very funny," he said. "I'm serious. Did anything stand out? Were there any odd visitors? Anyone watching you?"

I crossed my arms over my chest. "Like I said, the only odd visitor, the only odd person watching me, had been you."

"I guess that will remain a mystery for the time being." Cerros turned to me. "Are you sure you want to come?"

My mouth parted. Were we really talking about this again? How many times did I have to tell them I was going? "Yes," I said.

Cerros nodded. "And you know how to fight? You've gone through some training?"

I bit my lips. Not only had I never had any training, but I had also never even been in a fight. I wanted to answer truthfully, but was worried Thaniel would change his mind. Maybe the only reason he had agreed in the first place was that he assumed my parents had taught me some kind of self-defense.

Cerros exhaled loudly. "You're letting her go and she's had no formal training?"

"Why are you so surprised?" Thaniel asked, pushing off the wall he had been leaning against. "Her parents aren't Shadow Marked. In fact, that's why they left."

I let out the breath I had been holding, grateful that Thaniel was still supporting my decision. My parents would never want me to fight. But I would do what I had to in order to get them back.

Maybe if I had been trained to fight, I could have fought off the woman. Maybe I would have found Addie before she was taken. As these thoughts raced through me, I remembered the woman's proclamation: *"Where the poppy grows, discord sows."*

Images of the poppy field came to mind. Oddly, I longed for it. Could the saying be tied to the same field? If so, what did it mean?

I turned to Thaniel again. "Their saying, is it about the poppy field? Our poppy field?"

"Your poppy field?" Cerros asked, his eyebrow raised.

Thaniel ignored his brother. "That's where most of the bloodshed occurred when my grandfather overthrew Enley's grandfather."

"Are you going to tell her the rest?" Cerros asked. "If we're taking her, if she's going to live here one day, she needs to know."

My eyes widened. Cerros thought I was going to stay in Marwood? Why hadn't Thaniel told him? Was he worried he wouldn't help if he knew the truth? I bit my tongue to keep from blowing our cover. Instead, I focused on the question, wondering what "the rest" meant?

Thaniel held my gaze. "When you left, Enley used it against

our family. The decree had already been made public. He told our people that you couldn't bear to be with me."

My stomach sank. Enley was using me to cause strife within Marwood. He wanted the crown, and he was using my family to get it. My blood boiled.

Cerros crossed his arms over his chest. "I think the reason Enley wants you dead is two-fold. He wants to hurt Thaniel by taking away his fated. He also wants you to disappear so he can keep using you as a distraction, another reason for others to distrust our family. Thaniel's own fated wanted nothing to do with him."

I turned to Thaniel, feeling the shift in the room. Even if what Cerros said wasn't true, I was sure it hurt to hear. I swallowed, wondering if it was a good idea to go. I didn't know how to fight. I didn't know the land. Would I only be a hindrance?

But if I didn't go, if I didn't lead the charge, my parents and Addie were as good as dead.

I stood taller, straightening my back. "Teach me how to fight."

Cerros raised an eyebrow. "You think you can learn how to fight in one night?"

"We can teach her the basics." Thaniel turned to his brother. "No one will get close to her."

Cerros sighed. "I guess I'm in this by myself. You're going to be too busy watching her."

"He doesn't need to watch me," I said. "I'll be fine. Just show me a few moves."

As soon as the words were out of my mouth, Cerros was behind me. He wrapped his arm around my neck, pulling me backward. I hadn't been expecting it. His arm dug into my throat, closing the flow of air.

In an instant, Thaniel was by my side, pulling his brother off. I stumbled forward, gasping for breath.

"Lesson number one," Cerros said, "trust no one."

"That's not fair," I sputtered. "I wasn't expecting that."

Cerros rolled his eyes. "Lesson number two, nothing's fair in battle. Pay attention to your surroundings. Threats can come from anywhere."

I squared my shoulders, ready for the next attack. Behind me, I heard movement and turned to find Thaniel. I stepped to my left, and his hands met empty air. Before I could celebrate, Cerros swung his arm out and I ducked.

"That would have hurt!"

Cerros caught his balance. "Enley won't care if it hurts. Neither will his followers. They want you dead."

My stomach lurched. Hearing it so bluntly put the situation into perspective. Enley and his followers wanted me dead. The woman in White Bridge would have killed me if Thaniel hadn't been following me. I needed to pay better attention to my surroundings.

Somehow, I needed to become a trained fighter. In one night.

My body ached in places I never knew existed. My muscles were tight, screaming with each move I made. We had been practicing for hours and I was exhausted.

Thaniel reached for me, and I ducked. A swish of air tickled my face as his arm narrowly missed. He stumbled.

I stood, my eyes searching for Cerros. The hair on the back of my neck prickled, and I turned around. His eyes narrowed as he swung. I quickly stepped to my right, but wasn't fast enough. His clenched fist found my shoulder.

"Ouch," I moaned. "Can you be a little gentler?"

Thaniel stepped between me and his brother. He held his arm out, preventing Cerros from hitting me again. My hand flew to my shoulder, as if that would ease the pain.

Cerros pushed his brother away. "I didn't realize all we had to do was ask Enley to be gentler." He then turned to me. "No one's going to take it easy on you because you asked nicely."

I looked up. "You don't know that."

Cerros rolled his eyes. I knew it wasn't true. I knew he was right. No one would take it easy on me. The woman who had taken me from McLaughlin's had almost killed me. I shuddered, my eyes meeting Thaniel's as if sharing the same memory.

"No one will get close enough to hurt her," Thaniel muttered.

Now it was my turn to roll my eyes. "No. He's right. I have to be prepared. No one's going to take it easy on me."

Cerros adjusted the sleeve of his shirt, rolling it back down his arm. "We're set on our plan?"

In between our training sessions, we had come up with a plan to save my parents and Addie. Thaniel nodded. He didn't return my gaze, and my stomach sank. Was he having second thoughts? I needed him on my side. I needed his help if I was going to save them.

"I'll see you tomorrow," Cerros said.

With one last glance at his brother, he slipped into the hallway. The room was silent as I processed what we were going to do. Even though I was beyond thankful for Thaniel and Cerros, I was angry that I was even in the situation. I should be studying.

Thaniel's eyes met mine and my breath hitched. For just a moment, I wished we didn't have to leave. A part of me wanted to keep unraveling my memories, perhaps even give him a chance. Maybe I could be happy with him. He was so different from George—more intense, brooding even, but something pulled me closer.

Our connection was magnetic, unlike anything I had ever experienced. Every cell in my body wanted to be with him, to run my hands through his hair, to wrap my arms around his waist. But my head, my rational, logical self, kept me at bay.

"Are you ready?"

The question pulled me out of his orbit. I nodded.

He turned his back to me, and I looked around the room once more, wondering if I would ever see it again. Would I even see Thea again?

Thaniel opened the door. When he was sure the hallway was clear, he motioned me forward. I followed, my muscles protesting each step.

"Stay by my side," he instructed.

Dark shadows dipped across my vision, and I gripped his arm tightly, my nails digging into the skin. He didn't seem fazed but rather used the opportunity to pick up his pace. Now that I was holding his arm, he could guide me through the hallway quickly.

The castle was quiet, everyone asleep. My racing heart kept pace with our footfalls. I tried to calm my nerves, but the anxiety was eating away at me. I told myself it was normal. In the past twenty-four hours, I had been attacked by one of Enley's followers and nearly poisoned.

When we reached the main foyer, I loosened my grip on his arm. He opened the door, guiding me outside into the cool night. I wrapped my arms around my chest, trying to stay warm. Above us, the moon was bright, so much brighter than in White Bridge.

At the cottage, Scraps greeted us. I bent low, rubbing behind her ears. Thaniel cleared his throat, and I looked up. He gestured to the door, and I stood. We had a plan; we had to stick to it.

When we were inside, Thaniel locked the door behind us. He disappeared into his bedroom. Scraps sat at my feet, and I used the time to scratch her belly. Her eyes glazed over as another memory pushed itself forward.

I was standing in our field of poppies, waiting for Thaniel. The sun was high above me, and the breeze gently stirred the flowers. The memory faded, but I closed my eyes, pulling it back, dredging it from my subconscious little by little.

As the breeze wrapped around me, a tiny black ball of fur bounded forward. I stepped back, startled by its sudden appearance. The puppy jumped to my knees. I picked it up, brushing the matted fur. When it licked my cheek, I giggled.

"Are you going to pack?" Thaniel asked.

I opened my eyes, the memory fading. Scraps pawed at my arm, waiting for me to continue the belly rubs.

I stilled. I had found Scraps? I desperately wanted my memories. It wasn't fair that they had been stolen.

I turned to Thaniel. "I don't have anything to pack."

"The clothes Thea brought you?" He pinched the bridge of his nose. "Poppy, we have to leave. You need clothes."

I gave one final belly rub to Scraps. Inside his bedroom, Thaniel tossed a leather bag to me, and I quickly went through the clothes Thea had brought. I packed those I thought I could use, leaving behind the dress. I wouldn't need it where we were going.

When I finished, I sat on the bed. Scraps sat at my feet. I focused on her, willing another memory forward. When nothing came, I turned to Thaniel. "I found her. I was in the poppy field."

He nodded. "Is that all you remember?"

A tear slid down my cheek. I wanted to remember. I hated that there were memories hidden inside of me. Pieces of my younger self just waiting to be found. "I can't remember anything else," I answered. "I was waiting for you when she appeared from the forest."

Thaniel picked up his bag, slinging it over his shoulder. "You found her. You took her home that night, but your parents said she couldn't stay."

My stomach sank. That didn't seem right. My father loved dogs. Even though we hadn't had any pets, he always talked about his childhood dog. "Did you take her because they wouldn't let me keep her?"

He nodded. "I didn't even want her. I hate dogs."

I narrowed my eyes. "You hate dogs? Why?"

"I guess hate's a strong word," he said. "I strongly dislike dogs. When I was young, I was bit by one."

Scraps walked to Thaniel, her nails clicking on the floor. I didn't understand why he kept her if he disliked dogs so much. I searched my mind, trying to pull out another memory. The frustrating part was I knew they were there; I just couldn't access them. "Why did you keep her?"

He sighed. "You were so upset. You were worried she wouldn't make it on her own. Now I can't get rid of her."

His lips curved into a sly smile. I didn't know how to take his answer. Had he only taken her because of me? He obviously loved Scraps now; he had been joking that he couldn't get rid of her.

Thaniel moved to the door. I followed him outside. We slowly made our way into the night, following the tall fence.

When we reached the guard tower, Thaniel met Cullen. They talked quietly for only a moment. When Thaniel stepped away, Cullen opened the large wooden door.

A cool breeze wrapped around me when we stepped outside of the fence. I zipped my father's jacket, trying to keep warm.

Thaniel pressed something into Cullen's palm. "We'll meet you at the inn."

Cullen nodded. He closed the door behind us. I took a deep breath, inhaling the crisp night air.

By the time we reached the poppy field, I had only looked back once. The field of flowers stretched forward, beckoning me to my fate.

THANIEL

Doubt and fear crept forward, springing from the depths of me. Like the field of poppies, no matter how many times I pushed the feelings back, down into the abyss of my soul, they reappeared. When I'd burned the flowers, I believed it would set me free. Little did I know my chains were permanent.

What would happen when we rescued her parents? Could I handle losing her all over again?

Next to me, Poppy was quiet. I knew she wasn't ready for this. Her time in White Bridge had softened her. Her parents had managed stable jobs; they didn't struggle as they had in Marwood. She hadn't had to think about the possibility of fighting.

Cerros had been right. I was going to be preoccupied with her safety. I could only hope he would gather a few more soldiers. It would only be us, Cullen, and Lucien, who my father had sent out earlier to scout the Greys.

I had known Cullen for four years. He had been with me during my training with the army. He had been there when my curse was activated. During the attack, he had shielded me while the marks appeared, protecting me as my flesh burned. I didn't have many friends. It was easier without them, but I guess you could say Cullen was one of my closest.

When we finally came to the edge of the field, I led Poppy into the forest. As we stepped into its dark embrace the wind blew, shaking the leaves off of the surrounding trees. I powered on the tiny flashlight I kept in my pocket. I'd bought it in White Bridge, and it proved to be more useful than I ever imagined.

Since there was a traitor in our midst, we left before daybreak. I didn't want anyone to know our location. Cerros agreed to stay behind, to gather a few trusted soldiers and meet us. Then we would make our way to Greymoore Manor, Enley's home. I was sure he was holding Poppy's parents and friend there. Hopefully, the element of surprise was on our side.

A low howl echoed around us. I knew it was only one of the wild dogs and kept my pace. Poppy reached out, her hand brushing against my arm. My breath stilled.

"What was that?"

"Only the wild dogs," I answered. "Nothing to be concerned about."

Her arm fell to her side. I immediately felt the loss. I suppressed the urge to reach out and take her hand.

"Did I know about the decree?"

My stomach clenched. I didn't know the answer for certain. I had my suspicions. There had been rumors. If she knew, she hadn't been given the chance to stay. We were only kids, but I knew she felt the same way about me as I felt about her.

"I don't know," I finally answered. "As soon as I heard, I came for you."

She cleared her throat. "I remember our kiss. I remember wanting to be with you."

I swept the flashlight across our path. Even though this was what I had been waiting for, it didn't feel right.

"When you left to meet Princess Lara, I thought that would

be the last time I would see you," she continued. "I thought she was your fated. I remember feeling jealous. I didn't want to lose you."

"I knew she wasn't," I said. "Deep down, I always knew it was you."

That hadn't even been an exaggeration. It had always been Poppy.

"I wish I could remember more about my parents. I'm having a hard time believing they did this to me. I want my memories back, all of them."

I wanted the same thing. A part of me hoped that if she regained all of her memories, her feelings for me would return. The other part of me knew that five years had already passed. We were both very different people. The last time I had seen her, I had vowed that I would never activate my curse.

As the silence settled upon us, I said the only thing I could think of, "They'll come back. If you let them."

We had only been walking half an hour by the time we arrived at our first destination. The brick house loomed over us, casting disjointed shadows across the field from the light of the moon. Two large columns sat on either end of the front porch.

Thaniel walked up the stairs. I tried to summon his confidence, but my legs failed me. Besides the obvious nerves, I was exhausted. I gripped the railing, using it to guide me.

The front door opened, and a woman looked out. She smiled when she saw Thaniel. "I wasn't expecting you."

He stepped forward. "I have a favor. I need a place to stay, just until morning."

The woman nodded. "Of course. You know you're always welcome here."

He looked back, giving me a small smile.

When we were inside, the woman closed the door behind us, locking it. I bit my lips nervously, hoping we would be safe with his friend.

"The guest bedroom is through that hall," the woman said, pointing to her left. "You're welcome to stay as long as you like."

"Just the night," Thaniel repeated.

The woman looked at me. "I'm glad you found your way back to each other."

I shifted on my feet. She thought we were together—a couple. She must have pieced together that I was his fated. What she didn't realize was that I had little memory of Thaniel. She didn't know I was only on a mission to save my family.

The woman turned to Thaniel. "You'll find your happiness together. I've never been wrong. What I see always comes to pass."

My jaw slackened. I tried to make sense of what she said. All I knew was that we were staying with a family friend. How would she know we would find happiness? What an odd thing to say.

The woman's statement echoed in my ears, *"What I see always comes to pass."* My eyes widened, and I stepped backward. "Are you…"

"Poppy, this is Magmar Luce."

My jaw dropped. Thaniel hadn't warned me. When he said a family friend, I had to admit, I assumed it would be an older woman, a friend of his father's. Not the woman who had made Thaniel's decree. So many questions raced through me. "How do you make your predictions?" I asked.

Magmar Luce smirked, biting her lips. I wished I had just stayed silent. I hope I hadn't offended her.

"They're not predictions," she answered. "Come sit, and I'll answer your questions. I'll make tea."

I dropped my bag to the floor, grateful for the break from holding it. Thaniel led me into the sitting room. I sat on the couch. The cushion sank when he sat next to me.

When Magmar Luce joined us, she set two teacups on the small table in front of us. Hot steam curled into the air.

"Mint," Magmar Luce said, as if reading my mind.

I brought the cup to my lips, wondering how she knew what

I had been thinking. It must have been a lucky guess. Perhaps she was only being polite, letting us know the flavor proactively, before we had a chance to ask.

"How long have you known each other?" I lowered the cup from my lips. "You look so young, not at all what I was expecting."

"I've known Prince Thaniel's family for many years now," she answered, setting her cup on a table.

It still threw me off to hear Thaniel addressed as a prince. Even though I knew he was, it was easy to forget. He didn't act like one. I paused, my eyes drifting to my left, taking in the strands of hair that fell over his face, his muscles, his tattoos…

Magmar Luce cleared her throat. "I have to know. What were you expecting?"

I turned away from him. I guess I had been expecting an older woman. I wasn't even sure why; it had just been the first thing that came to mind. I silently debated the best way to answer. I didn't want to offend her. "I guess I had been expecting someone older," I answered slowly, searching for the right words. "I'm not sure why."

Her eyes met mine. "Sometimes our preconceived notions only hold us back. Let go of those that do not serve you."

I held her gaze for only a moment. Her clear green eyes drilled into mine. It felt as if she was searching, reading me from the outside in. My heart hammered in my chest, and I turned away, trying to play it off as if I needed to readjust myself to get comfortable.

"I have to say," Magmar Luce continued, "it surprised me to read that you're Thaniel's fated."

I clasped my hands, resting them on my lap. What was so surprising about us being fated? My background? That my family was poor and Thaniel was a prince? That he was Shadow Marked?

"Only because you had been friends for so long," Magmar

Luce continued. "From what I gather, you were friends for three years before the decree?"

"Four," Thaniel spoke up. "We had been friends for four years prior."

The hair on my arm prickled at his voice. I looked away, my eyes searching the room, a distraction from the thoughts overtaking me.

Magmar Luce nodded. "That's unusual. I'm only surprised I hadn't picked up on it sooner."

What did that mean? My mind turned over the possibilities. Did she practice magic? Is that how she made the connections? Next to me, Thaniel shifted in his seat.

"I come from a long line of magmars. Your connection, your bond, is the strongest I've ever felt."

My eyes met Thaniel's. He held my gaze. Suddenly, the distance between us felt too big. I took a deep breath, trying to think clearly. What was happening to me?

I turned to Magmar Luce. "What do you mean, the strongest you ever felt? How do you know his fated? Are you Shadow Marked as well?"

She picked up her tea. "No, I'm not Shadow Marked. My family has worked with Prince Thaniel's for quite some time though. I feel the bond. I can sense it."

"I'm still confused," I said. "Is it magic? What brings us together?"

"It's part of our curse," Thaniel answered. "We'll never be truly happy until we find our other half. My grandfather hired Magmar Luce's family to help."

Magmar Luce nodded. "We can sense the bonds. We tap into the energy, the magic around us."

I sighed. I still didn't understand. Maybe I never would.

If the Shadow Marked would never be truly happy until they found their fated, what did that mean for Thaniel? I didn't know if I wanted to be with him. It was too much pressure.

Magmar Luce shifted in her seat, her eyes meeting Thaniel's. "We all thought you'd be fated to the princess."

My skin tingled. She was referring to Princess Lara. I hadn't been happy with the thought back then, and for some reason, it angered me now. I didn't know if I even wanted to be with him, but that didn't mean I wanted him with someone else.

I stood. "Please excuse me, I'm exhausted. Thank you for your hospitality."

Thaniel stood, but I didn't wait for him. I stepped into the hallway. As I passed, I picked up my bag. I spent little time looking around the house. I made a beeline for the bedroom, more than ready to put the day behind me.

When I was alone, I dropped the bag on the floor. I ran my hands through my hair, trying to calm the confusion that had been building. A shiver passed through me. I didn't have to turn around to know Thaniel had joined me.

He leaned close, whispering into my ear, "Don't be jealous of Princess Lara. You can have me whenever you want."

Breath caught in my throat. Sweat pooled at my neck as his words replayed in my head, sending shivers down my spine. I closed my eyes, trying to pull myself together. I slowly turned, my heart hammering in my chest. Would he kiss me? Did I want him to kiss me?

He closed the door. He pulled his shirt over his head, revealing toned abs. The tattoos snaked their way up his chest, toward his neck. I wanted to tell him to put his shirt back on, but the words wouldn't come. Instead, I quickly made my way to the bed, pulling the covers up to my chin. He turned off the lights and lay on a large sofa near the windows.

As I closed my eyes, the truth hit me. I wanted him. Like a moth to a flame, our bond was intense, and I didn't know if I was strong enough to break free.

POPPY

FIVE YEARS AGO

The rain fell so hard I couldn't see anything more than a few feet away. From my shelter underneath the tree, I waited, hoping for a break. Thaniel had left a while ago when the storm had only just begun. I should have left when he did. I had hoped it would pass quickly, but now I realized that had been a mistake.

The wind picked up, blowing so fiercely I feared my new dress would tear. I bunched the fabric in my fists, hoping to keep it contained. I'd only had it a day.

When the tree branches swayed in the wind, cold rainwater wrapped around me. I brought my hands to my chest, trying to stay warm. I debated making a run for it. The water was already on me. What did it matter now?

My eyes scanned the fence, wondering if Thaniel would return. A part of me didn't want to leave. Perhaps he would meet Princess Lara and come back for me. I would brave the rain for another moment with him.

I wanted to hear everything about the princess. I needed to hear that they weren't fated. I knew I was being ridiculous. Even if he wasn't fated to her, he would find his match...and it wouldn't be me.

I had to find a way to control my emotions, to quell the expectations. Growing up, I was told that the right person would come my way. My parents used to tell me I would marry and have a family of my own. They liked to tell me I would be happy. Had that been a lie? Just something parents told their children, a delusion they created to make the pain of everyday life manageable? I didn't feel happy. I didn't think I ever would.

When the bells rang, my blood chilled. They cut through me, a knife to the heart. The bell tower sat high above the hill behind the castle. They were only used for one thing, to alert the kingdom when one of their own, a Shadow Marked, found their fated love.

The decrees were usually a joyous occasion, full of celebration. In my heart, I knew the decree was for Thaniel. My stomach churned at the thought that I may never see him again.

A single tear fell down my cheek, and I quickly wiped it away. I would be strong. I wanted him to be happy. Even if it wasn't with me.

Before I lost my nerve, I stepped into the storm. My heart hammered in my chest as I ran, my feet sinking into the wet grass. The rain pierced me, leaving small red marks on my skin. Another gust of wind wrapped around me, but I pushed forward. I had to know.

Only when I reached the castle gate did I stop. My wet hair clung to my face. Even my eyelashes were soaked, tiny drops of water coating them. I held my hand over my eyes, trying to see. If I could find a soldier, I could ask about the decree. There wouldn't be a formal announcement until tomorrow, but surely, they had to know. The prince's decree would be the talk of the castle.

A low rumble of thunder echoed around me. I knew I should go home. I was freezing, and my new dress was ruined, but all thoughts of leaving left when the castle gate swung open. I ran forward, dodging puddles of water.

When my father appeared, I stopped. For a moment, neither of us moved, both wondering what the other was doing. Another low rumble of thunder brought us back to the moment. He ran toward me as the gate closed behind him.

I looked up at the castle. What was Thaniel doing right now? Was he with Princess Lara? Was he happy? Had he already forgotten about me?

"What are you doing out here?" my father asked. "You should be home."

I met his gaze. "It's Thaniel, isn't it?"

At his silence, I knew the answer. My arms fell to my sides. How was I supposed to go on now?

He sighed. "We'll talk about it at home."

I nodded. He took my hand, and I followed. The storm continued to rage on, but I was thankful. At least it hid my tears.

The room was empty when I awoke. Where was Thaniel? Flashes of the dream appeared before me. It was beginning to seem as if I hadn't known that the decree had been of me. From the memories that were slowly returning, I had been falling in love with him.

I threw the blanket off and stood, elongating my spine and stretching my neck. I missed my bed. I missed the comfort of my home in White Bridge.

I shuffled to the door, opening it slowly. Voices carried from the living room. My footfalls were quiet as I made my way down the hall.

"Are you going to tell her?" Magmar Luce asked.

"No," Thaniel's sharp voice answered quickly. "She'll remember everything when she's ready."

She sighed. "The way you're acting, it's as if you have no real attachment to her. Maybe I was wrong, maybe you're both destined for others. Your connection is so strong, but maybe you aren't meant to be."

I held my breath, waiting to hear Thaniel's reply. The house was silent, as if on bated breath as well. Maybe that's why I didn't feel the overwhelming need to be with him. Sure, he was handsome and there had been feelings at one point—my memories proved that—but he was brooding, Shadow Marked, not at all what I pictured my future partner to be. Could Magmar Luce have been wrong?

"I'll kill anyone who touches her," Thaniel muttered. "It's bad enough I had to sit by and watch her with her ex. I can't do it again."

"Then tell her," Magmar Luce said. "I don't understand why you're helping. They took her from you, against her will. We heard what happened."

I swallowed. That answered that question. I knew the decree had been of me. I couldn't believe my parents forced me to leave before I could talk to him. Something was placed on a table, the sound making me jump. When I was sure they hadn't heard me, I crept closer, waiting for Thaniel's reply.

"We don't know for certain," he finally said. "There will always be rumors."

"Either way, they knew, and they took her. They didn't give you a chance."

His reply was quiet. "They did what they thought was right at the time. I had tried to show them I was different, but I guess in the end, my marks prove they were right."

"You and Cerros are different. You're Shadow Marked, but you're not like the rest of them. They crave it, the two of you..."

They were then silent.

My thoughts overtook me. Thaniel had killed before. Not only did his marks prove it, but I had witnessed it. Even though he had done it to protect me, it was an odd feeling to know that he had taken a life.

I turned, preparing to make my way back to the bedroom, when the floorboards creaked underneath me. Before I could move, Thaniel was behind me. I opened my mouth, but words failed me. Should I tell him I heard everything? Do I thank him for helping me save my parents, even though they separated us?

"We're leaving," he said. "We have to meet Cerros. Get your things."

I nodded before quickly making my way to the bedroom. I ran my fingers over my forehead, trying to come to terms with the strange turn of events in my life. This isn't how I envisioned my weekend.

After I gathered my few belongings, I met Thaniel in the hall. He hadn't moved. He was leaning against the wall, his arms hanging limply at his sides. His blond hair was loose around his face.

His eyes followed me. "Do you have everything?"

I pointed to my bag. "Yes."

Magmar Luce joined us. She pushed a beige napkin in my hands, wrapping my fingers around it.

"Berlberry bread."

I adjusted the napkin, revealing a bread speckled with blue fruit. It looked like blueberry bread, and my stomach rumbled. "Blueberry bread?"

She cocked her head. "Berlberry. Have you forgotten them too?"

I recovered the bread. One more thing to add to the list of forgotten memories. Magmar Luce led us to the door. When she opened it, she stepped back, allowing us to pass.

"Be careful," she said. "There've been reports of—"

"Thank you," Thaniel interrupted, stepping past her.

I clutched the bread in my hands, tightening my fingers around the napkin. A shudder crept down my back as I remembered the large cat-like creature we encountered on our way to the castle. What else did this land hold? What other creatures were out there?

I followed Thaniel, but Magmar Luce reached for my hand. Her icy touch gave me pause. I stopped, turning to face her.

"Stay with Thaniel," she warned. "If you leave him, if you separate…"

Her words sent another chill down my spine.

She closed her eyes, as if trying to see the vision. A shadow fell over us. I looked up to find Thaniel. His eyes met mine, a thought passing between us. Was she seeing my death? Would our rescue mission end in tragedy? I held my breath, waiting for her to continue.

When she opened her eyes, she shook her head. "I can't see it."

I removed my hand from her tight grip. I clenched my fingers, my nerves rattled.

"You can't see anything because nothing's going to happen," Thaniel said. "I won't let her out of my sight."

I exhaled; grateful his resolve hadn't swayed. He was still going to help me.

Magmar Luce stepped back toward the house. Thaniel took my hand and led me forward, into the unknown.

POPPY

For someone who hadn't been worried about the vision, Thaniel kept pace with me, barely letting me out of his reach. We hadn't been walking long. After leaving Magmar Luce's house, we followed a path into the forest. As we walked, I thought of my parents. A part of me was mad that they had lied to me for so long. How could I forgive that?

My stomach rumbled, and I unwrapped the napkin. I brought the berlberry bread to my nose.

Thaniel stopped walking, his eyebrow raised. "What's wrong?"

I gestured to the bread. "Is this safe to eat?"

He led me around a large clump of brush. I broke a piece of the bread. It crumbled in my fingers. I brought it to my lips, waiting for his answer.

When he turned to me, his face lit up. "You don't remember the berlberry bread I made? I'm actually glad it was so forgettable. I didn't think I would ever live that down."

I placed the crumble of bread on the napkin again. "You bake?"

"No." He chuckled. "The one time I did hadn't worked out so well."

I pushed a thin tree branch out of my way. "I feel like there's a story here. What happened? Did you give everyone food poisoning?"

He smiled, his lips curled, revealing his teeth. From my short time with him, it didn't seem as if he smiled much in his day-to-day life. It was infectious.

"Only us," he answered sheepishly. "Oh, and Thea."

I nodded. His answer hadn't surprised me. He didn't strike me as someone who enjoyed baking. He was a prince.

My eyes fell on his tattoos again, reminding me he was also a killer. What would he need to bake for?

"That's safe to eat," he added, pointing to the bread in my hand. "I had some earlier."

My mouth salivated at the thought of the bread. Would berlberries taste like blueberries? Would it make me sick? I didn't remember having them before. I picked up the broken piece and brought it to my mouth. I was so hungry I placed it on my tongue without another thought.

The sweetest taste filled me. Hints of vanilla, sugar, and the sweet fruit shocked my tastebuds. I quickly broke off another piece.

"We're almost at the meeting place. Everything's going according to plan."

I looked up, brushing the napkin free of crumbs. When it was clear, I folded it and placed it in my pocket. It could come in useful on our journey.

"Don't jinx us," I said. "Everyone always says that before disaster strikes."

He raised his hand over his eyes, looking into the distance. "I make my own fortune."

"You think it works like that?"

"I know it does."

I didn't know if I agreed with his optimism. I had more of a don't-tempt-fate thought process. Now that he put that out there, spoke the words out loud, was our destiny sealed? My eyes darted first to the left and then the right, looking for any threats.

Magmar Luce's warning rang in my head, and I stepped closer to Thaniel, nearly touching his arm. He pointed to the right, toward a dark section of forest. Massive trees grew around us, their giant leaves keeping the light from reaching the ground.

I held my arm out, preventing him from moving forward. "Are you sure we should go in there?"

"That's the way to the lake," he answered, his voice even. "Cerros is meeting us there."

I bit my lips, the cracked, dry skin another reminder that we weren't in White Bridge. I wanted my lip balm. I wanted a cup of coffee. I wanted to feel safe again. I wanted my parents.

"Are you sure it's safe? It's really dark in there."

He stepped around my hand. "We'll be fine."

I followed him into the dark, staying at his side. I didn't know if the magmar's warning had only been a bad feeling, or a vision of the future. Either way, I didn't want to find out. I was going to stay at his side.

We walked in silence. Occasionally, a few leaves fell from the tall trees. I strained my eyes in the dark forest, searching for the lake. I knew the plan was to meet Cerros at Lake Trenmont. They had picked the lake because it was deep in the forest, away from prying eyes. From the way they talked, no one lived near the lake, a fact that I now verified.

In the distance, a soft yellow glow lit up the darkness. I watched the light, wondering if Thaniel saw it too. Before I could ask, more appeared, each a different color. Soft green, blue, pink, and purple joined the yellow, lighting the way and reflecting off the water. The lake was calm, the water still.

My eyes darted from each color before me. "What are the glowing lights? They're beautiful."

He didn't miss a beat. "Don't touch them. They're poisonous. They're a type of mushroom."

He stepped onto a wooden bridge. The magmar's warning rang through me once more and I followed. I scanned the edge of the large lake, looking for Cerros. I was anxious to continue the journey to save my family. My stomach dropped as I thought of Addie. Her parents must be so worried about her.

When the walkway widened, Thaniel stopped. He leaned over the railing; his head dipped to look into the water. I took a deep breath, and wrapped my arms around my chest, studying our surroundings for anything out of place, any danger waiting in the dark.

"When we find them," I began, my voice cracking. "I haven't changed my mind. I'm going home."

He stood but didn't answer. I looked away, inhaling deeply. A strong cedar scent overwhelmed me.

"I know," he finally said. "A part of me hopes you'll change your mind." He turned to me, his eyes meeting mine. "I keep thinking all of your memories will come back and you'll want to stay...you'll want to be with me."

The air was thick, hot, and muggy, as I contemplated the best way to answer. What could I say to that? I didn't know if I would even remember everything. What I had remembered was more than I was ready to face. I swallowed, words failing me yet again.

He stepped forward, so close he took my breath away. Images of the last memory overtook me. The rain had been so cold it burned my skin.

"They're coming back...slowly," I choked out.

He reached forward, tucking a strand of hair behind my ear. My breath caught in my throat. At that moment, the rest of the world fell away. I couldn't imagine being away from him. The thought hurt.

He leaned close, his voice sending shivers down my spine, "I can be patient."

I looked up, our eyes meeting. His lips parted, and something overcame me. I wrapped my arms around his neck, pulling him close.

His breath was warm on my skin. I ran my hands through his hair, twisting a strand around my finger. He placed his palm on my cheek, leaning in even closer. His touch made my knees weak, and I wrapped my arms around him tighter.

I closed my eyes as our lips met, losing myself in his strong grip. He wrapped his arms around the small of my back, pulling me so close it felt as if he were on top of me. A fire in my belly raged, and I groaned. I didn't want the moment to end. My heart raced so fast I couldn't think clearly.

George had never kissed me like this.

Too soon, he pulled away. He placed his head on my forehead, his breath ragged. I fought the urge to run my hands through his hair again, to reach up and brush my lips against his.

"Are you done?" a voice called.

Thaniel's hands moved to his side. In a flash, his dagger appeared.

I turned, relieved to find Cerros. He was leaning against a tree, his arms crossed over his chest.

"I see your memories are coming back," he said, looking at me before turning to Thaniel. "I thought you'd be smarter. We have enemies. Now's not the time."

Thaniel placed the dagger in its sheath. "What took you?"

"The usual," he answered, almost bored. "Father didn't want to send anyone."

Thaniel's brow furrowed. I ran the back of my hand over my lips, as if trying to wipe away the kiss. How had I lost myself in his embrace so easily? I had to find my parents. I had to find Addie. What had I been thinking?

Cerros pushed off the tree. "Let's go."

Thaniel looked away, almost as if he shared my sentiment. Had he realized what a mistake it had been?

He gestured me off the bridge. "After you."

My mouth ran dry. I had to push my feelings away. Somehow, they had been erased, covered by the veil of magic. At that moment, I didn't want them back. I didn't want the distraction.

THANIEL

What had I been thinking? I shouldn't have kissed Poppy. Now wasn't the time. She barely had any memories of me.

While I could be patient, I didn't know how much longer I even had with her. My eyes focused on the back of her head. She stepped off the bridge, making her way toward Cerros. While I was happy to see him, the timing hadn't been ideal.

"How many did you get?" I called.

Cerros exhaled. "Not enough. Cullen will bring them to the inn."

I nodded.

Poppy stopped a few feet from my brother. She crossed her arms over her chest, avoiding all eye contact with me.

I wished I could hear her thoughts. I suppressed the urge to run to her, to wrap her in my arms. I would give anything to be lost in her kiss again.

When I stepped off the bridge, Cerros joined me.

"I passed a group of hunters beyond the lake," he said. "We should leave."

"Hunters?" Poppy asked. "What're those?"

"I believe you have them in White Bridge." He chuckled. "People that hunt wild game. I don't think they'll be a problem." His eyes met mine. "But you can never be too careful."

I looked away. I didn't need his condescending attitude. Like true siblings, he liked to hold things over me. Because he was the heir, the next in line to the throne, he liked to believe that he was smarter than me, that he knew better.

I wasn't in the mood. I bit my lips to keep from answering. Even though we were close, and he was always there for me, he still grated on my nerves like no other.

"Seriously?" Cerros said. "What were you thinking?"

Poppy turned to face me, waiting to hear my answer. While it hadn't been the smartest move, anyone could have snuck up on us, I wouldn't take it back. I had been waiting five years for that kiss.

"I was thinking I finally found my fated."

Cerros rolled his eyes and Poppy turned away. I adjusted the bag over my shoulder, pushing aside all thoughts. I needed to refocus. The marks on my chest vibrated softly, excited for what was to come.

POPPY

e were still walking as the sun began its descent. For a moment, I wondered if it was the same sun I was used to seeing in White Bridge. Was that even possible? Could our very different worlds rotate around the same celestial object?

Maybe we weren't as different after all.

The silence was grating on my nerves. I hadn't spoken to Thaniel since Cerros joined us after our kiss. The way his hands brought me close, pressing his body into mine, made my knees weak. Just the thought sent a shockwave of desire through me. More than once, I caught myself looking at him, wondering what he was thinking. His expression unyielding the clues I had been searching for.

I wrapped my arms around my chest as the temperature dropped. To the left, a branch snapped. I turned but didn't see anything. Thaniel and Cerros didn't seem phased, and I knew it was only an animal, or the wind, but my mind wouldn't stop wandering, making up all sorts of scary scenarios.

Cerros turned to look at me. "So, you're finally beginning to remember?"

I stepped over a small puddle; the water cloudy with dirt. "Just small pieces. Not everything."

My eyes darted to Thaniel, hoping to see his reaction. He kept his gaze straight. His shoulders relaxed—the only indication he had been listening.

"Well, I hope the rest of your memories come back soon," Cerros said. "You have to take him off my hands."

"Ha-ha," Thaniel said, bending down and picking up a clump of moss. He rolled it in his palms, forming a ball before launching it at his brother.

Cerros let out a yelp of surprise when the moss hit his back. I pressed my lips together, their banter surprising. Cerros launched himself at his brother, trying to lock him into his firm grip. Thaniel easily removed himself and their laughter echoed.

I narrowed my eyes, wondering if they had both lost their minds. Why were they making so much noise? Having been an only child, I wasn't used to the sibling dynamic. For a moment, I let my mind wander, imagining a brother or sister to share my life with.

"Did you figure out who poisoned Thea?" I asked, my question breaking up their play.

At the mention of their sister, both Thaniel and Cerros stilled. They stepped away from each other.

Finally, Cerros shook his head. "No. There were more people than normal in the kitchen that night. We can't pinpoint who had access to the food."

"She's doing better?" Thaniel asked. "You said she was. You wouldn't lie to me, right?"

"When I left, she was up and walking around," Cerros answered. "She's doing much better."

Thaniel's eyes met mine. I offered him a strained smile, hoping to convey my sympathy. Instead of being with his sister, he was with me, on the hunt for my parents and Addie. My stomach sank when I realized he wasn't even getting anything out of it. I had told him I was going back to White Bridge, away from him.

"She'll be back to herself in time for the Recendence," Cerros added a little too cheerfully. "Now that your memories are coming back, I imagine it will only be a matter of time."

Thaniel turned away from me. When he didn't say anything, I turned to Cerros. "What's the Recendence?"

The smile fell from his face. "You don't remember?"

I was getting tired of everyone asking me that. *No, I don't remember anything*, I wanted to scream.

Before I could answer, Thaniel spoke, "She's going back to White Bridge. After we rescue her family. She isn't staying."

Cerros raised his eyebrow, as if he couldn't quite believe his brother. I crossed my arms over my chest, angry that they wouldn't answer me. Above us, a bat-like creature flew by, its wings spread wide.

"Will one of you tell me what that is? Do I need to be worried about something else?"

"No, you don't have to worry about it," Thaniel said. "It's a ceremony."

I didn't think I heard him. A ceremony? Why would I be participating in a ceremony? My thoughts turned, trying to make sense of what they were hinting at.

"It's a ceremony that usually happens right after the decree," Cerros said quickly. "Letting the kingdom know that both parties have accepted the pairing. Forget I mentioned it."

I pinched the bridge of my nose. Why did everything keep coming back to the decree? Beside me, Thaniel shifted on his feet. Movement out of the corner of my eye drew my attention. I gasped as a large green-and-brown snake, speckled with round eye-like circles, slithered by our feet. It was the largest snake I had ever seen. I fell backward. When I landed on the rough ground, a shockwave of pain ran up my body.

Thaniel held his arm to me, inviting me to take it. "It won't hurt you."

I brushed him away, standing up quickly in case there were more. Snakes were not at the top of my list of favorite animals.

"There's a nest of them," Cerros said, pointing to our left, past a large tree. "I can see it."

There were more? An icy shiver went through me as I stepped closer to Thaniel, hoping his protection extended to snakes.

"Remember when we used to hunt them?" Thaniel asked.

I narrowed my eyes. "You must be mistaken."

He chuckled. "I'm not. We used to look for their nests. You used to collect the blue stones found in their shells."

My jaw dropped. "I would never go near a snake nest."

He shifted the bag on his shoulder. "You had quite the collection. You were going to make a necklace."

I couldn't imagine myself chasing snakes or digging in their nests. It just didn't seem like anything I would do. What else was I going to learn about myself?

Another chill went through me. Maybe the past was better left forgotten.

POPPY

After the revelation about snake hunting, I wondered if I even knew myself. It was so out of character I still wondered if Thaniel was mistaking me for someone else. I couldn't picture myself going anywhere near a snake pit, digging inside the nest. I couldn't picture myself wanting to wear a necklace of stones found in their shells.

Thaniel stepped closer to me, pointing to our left. "Stay away from the water."

Even before the warning, I didn't want to go anywhere near the large bog. Rotten tree trunks climbed through the surface, their broken limbs appearing from the murky depths. Large green lily pads covered the middle, leaving only the sides open to the elements.

"I'm not going anywhere near that," I said. "But why? What's in there?"

"Illarians."

My heart sped up. I glanced at the water again. What were Illarians? I looked back at Thaniel.

"Mermaids?" I asked. "Are there mermaids living in there?"

"They're not the fairytale mermaids you're thinking of," Cerros said.

My eyes wandered to the water again. Had they met one before? Even though the curiosity was eating away at me, I hoped we wouldn't see one. The huge cat-like creature we had encountered on our way to Marwood had been traumatizing enough.

Cerros turned back to Thaniel. "What's the plan when we get there?"

The question caught my attention. "Will everyone be there? Do you think they'll have an idea where my parents are being held?"

"One question at a time," Thaniel said. He turned to his brother. "The plan is to get to the inn and wait for Lucien. Hopefully, he knows if Enley is still at Greymoore Manor." He then turned to me. "Cullen should be there shortly after we arrive."

A sharp barking drew my attention. A small brown and white dog was yipping at the edge of the bog, looking into the water. When it heard us, it turned around and shook its tail, waving it wildly back and forth.

A pale, wrinkled hand shot out of the water. My breathing stilled as long, boney fingers clamped on the dog's fur. It let out another sharp yelp and struggled at the surface, clawing at something unseen.

My feet propelled me forward. I had to help. When I reached the edge, the dog was still struggling to remain above water. I stepped into the ice-cold bog.

Behind me, Thaniel screamed my name. My ears thrummed from the adrenaline, and I couldn't make sense of what he was saying. Suddenly, the dog swam toward the edge, released from whatever had it in its hold.

A low shiver went through me when something slimy

brushed against my leg. Thaniel jumped into the bog as I was pulled under. Water went up my nose as I frantically inhaled, caught unaware. I opened my eyes, and my blood ran cold. Before me was a monster. I scrambled backward, trying to put as much distance as I could between myself and the thing before me.

When I reached the surface, I inhaled deeply, filling my lungs with much-needed air. A hand clamped on my right arm, pulling me toward the shore. I looked up to find Thaniel when something gripped my leg again. I only had a moment before it pulled me back under.

I inhaled the murky water. My lungs burned. Before me was a mermaid, only it didn't look like the mermaid from any fairy-tale I had read. The monster before me was tall, covered in gray, flaky skin. Pea-green hair framed the wrinkled face, and pale red eyes bore into mine.

I paddled my arms backward, trying to swim away, but it held me in its tight grip. My heart rate increased, and my lungs burned. I longed to open my mouth, to breathe in the fresh air. The mermaid ran a hand along my cheek, scratching me with its long nails. I flung my arms forward, but my advances were useless.

The mermaid smiled, revealing large razor-sharp teeth. She caught my arms easily, wrapping her hands over mine. A thin, forked tongue shot out of her mouth and landed on my cheek. Everything within me screamed to get away, but I was trapped.

When the mermaid's tongue grazed against my cheek again, my stomach dropped. Where was Thaniel? He had been next to me moments ago. The monster's eyes bore into mine as she leaned close and placed her mouth against my neck. Her lips wrapped around my flesh and her sharp teeth bit into me, tearing the skin.

Strong arms wrapped around me, pulling me to the surface. Out of the corners of my eyes, I saw Cerros wielding a large knife. Bright red blood pooled around us, painting the water.

A moment later, fresh air greeted me. I gasped for breath, feeling it glide into my lungs. Thaniel dragged me to the bank, lifting me easily.

"Get away from the edge," he commanded. "I have to help."

I nodded; my body was too numb to speak. I slowly crawled forward, away from the water. When a splash filled the silence, I closed my eyes, fear eating away at me. Had the mermaid come back for me? Could she come out of the water?

My fingers dug into the dirt as I continued forward, too scared to turn around. Each movement was painful. I opened my mouth, inhaling the air like it was my last. A low whimper sounded to my right. I looked up, surprised to find the dog at the base of a tree. Its eyes were trained on me, watching from a distance.

Behind me, I heard the sound of splashing water. I turned, relieved to see Thaniel and Cerros. Water dripped down their bodies and pooled at their feet. Thaniel immediately made his way to me.

"What happened to her?" I asked, my voice trembling. "Can she come out of the water?"

Thaniel knelt before me. He reached out and ran his hand down my cheek, stopping on my neck, where the mermaid had bitten me. I closed my eyes, savoring his touch.

"I told you to stay out of the water," he growled. "What were you thinking?"

My eyes flew open. Was he serious? Hadn't he seen the dog? I held my arm out, pointing to the dog at the base of the tree. His eyes didn't leave mine.

"I don't care about the dog," he said. "You could have been killed."

His fingers slid across my skin gently, and I swallowed. The air around us electrified, as if at any moment his touch would ignite me.

Cerros stepped forward, wringing the water out of his shirt. "We should go. More will come when they smell the blood."

"What happened to her?" I asked.

Thaniel helped me sit before answering, "She's dead. He's right though, more will come. They're attracted to the blood."

I bit my lips, remembering the mermaid's teeth on my neck. She was going to kill me.

"Don't do that again," Thaniel said. "You heard the magmar's warning."

I looked back at the tree. Relief washed through me when I saw the dog. When our eyes met, it wagged its tail before darting toward me. A rough, wet tongue slid across my arm. I ran my hand across its head, scratching behind the ears.

"I couldn't let that thing get him," I said.

Thaniel stood. He opened his mouth as if he were going to disagree, but I didn't care. Even though I knew it hadn't been my smartest move, I had to do something. I couldn't let that monster kill it.

"Are you able to walk?" Thaniel asked.

I moved the dog off of my lap and stood. Even though my legs were shaky, I felt okay. I had survived a mermaid attack. I couldn't wait to tell Addie everything I had been through. My stomach sank. I hoped I would see her soon.

The dog nipped at my heels. I knelt, scratching behind its ears again.

"What are we going to do with him?"

"Leave him," Cerros scoffed. "What would you like to do with him?"

"Poppy, we can't take him with us," Thaniel added. "He'll be okay."

I knew he was right. We couldn't take the dog with us. We were on a quest to save my parents and Addie. I didn't need one more thing to worry about, another distraction.

I brought my arms around my chest, trying to keep warm

when I heard the splash of water. Two pale, red eyes stared back at me. Another mermaid had joined the first.

At my feet, the dog whimpered. Thaniel took my hand and led me away from the water. Cerros stepped around me, leading us deeper into the forest. Thaniel shook his head when the dog followed, but didn't say anything.

Even though it wasn't smart to take the dog, to take on the responsibility when I just wanted to save my family, I wasn't going to stop it from following us. Besides, he was just as lost as I was, and I couldn't shake the feeling that I was meant to find him.

I turned to Thaniel, realizing that I was having the same thoughts about him. I was meant to reunite with him. As much as it scared me, I was meant to be by his side.

POPPY

FIVE YEARS AGO

The rain fell all around us, ice-cold and hard. I held my arms above my head, trying to protect myself from the sharp drops. My feet ached as we ran, dodging large puddles and others caught in the storm. My father darted ahead, turning at the large weeping cherry tree. We followed the path toward our house as my mind raced.

The day I had worried about for so long finally arrived. Thaniel had his decree. I would never see him again.

The front door opened, and my mother peered out. "Hurry!"

We bounded up the stairs and into the house. When we were inside, my mother closed the door as a loud boom of thunder shook me to my core. We hadn't been expecting rain. Where had it come from?

"Dinner's ready," my mother said cheerfully, her eyes falling to me. "Poppy, your new dress is wet. Why are you crying?"

I ran my hands under my eyes, wiping the tears. I didn't even care that my dress was wet. There were bigger things to think about.

"You heard the bells?" my father asked.

My mother's hands fell to her sides. She looked at me, and her face softened. "Poppy...You knew this would happen. You can't be with him."

Another fresh batch of tears fell. I couldn't stop them. Even though she had been right, I knew I would never be with him, it still hurt.

My father exhaled loudly. "It's Poppy. Thaniel's decree. It's Poppy," he repeated.

I turned to face him. Even though I heard the words, they weren't making sense. Could it be real? Had it really been me? The Universe had finally sent me its favor. I wouldn't have to worry about marrying someone I didn't love. I was going to be with Thaniel.

"It's me?" I asked, the words barely audible. "Really?"

"I was in the castle," my father said, taking my mother's hands. "I think you should sit."

I stepped forward; my legs shaky. Water dripped off of me, pooling at my feet, but I didn't care. Why did he sound like this was a bad thing? Wasn't he excited? We wouldn't have to worry about anything ever again. Thaniel would take care of us. Not only would he want to, but he would have to.

I was his fated. I could hardly believe it.

My father led my mother to the large chair near the door. Even though the cushion was ripped, and the frame was scuffed, it was my mother's favorite. She always said it brought back fond memories of her childhood. It had been passed down through her family for years.

But I knew the truth. They couldn't afford any other furniture. She had grown to love it out of necessity. The chair groaned when she sat.

"How?" she asked, her face pale. "It can't be Poppy. We have to leave. If we go now, we can disappear before he comes for her."

My parents continued their conversation as if I wasn't even there. It didn't matter, though; I couldn't even follow along. My ears pulsed with a heartbeat of their own. The room spun, and I grasped for something to keep me upright. This didn't make sense. Why weren't they happy?

My mother flew from the chair, making her way to the kitchen. My father followed, talking over my mother's frantic panic. I stood silent and still, their words circling me.

Suddenly, my mother was before me. She placed her hands on my shoulders. "This isn't a good thing, Poppy. They're not good people."

I snapped out of my stupor. The room came back into focus, and I blinked, trying to ground myself.

My voice cracked when I finally answered, "I don't understand."

Her hand flew to her forehead, and she rubbed her temple. "They're Shadow Marked. This isn't a good thing." She turned on my father. "We should have put a stop to this a long time ago. We shouldn't have accepted the dress."

I ran my hand along the fabric when the weight of their conversation hit me. *"We shouldn't have accepted the dress."*

"What does that mean?"

My father rubbed underneath his eyes, as if trying to smooth away the dark bags. He exhaled loudly as my mother sat again. Outside, the rain continued to fall, hitting the roof and echoing around us.

"Did Thaniel give you the dress to give to me?" I asked. As soon as the words were out of my mouth, I knew it was true. My parents couldn't afford it. I had been naïve. Even though my father had been working more, we weren't in a position to buy anything other than necessities. Why hadn't anyone told me?

"He's Shadow Marked," my mother said. "You don't want to be caught up in that."

"He's not like the rest of them," I protested. "He won't activate the curse."

My mother raised her eyebrow, narrowing her eyes at me. "You're young, Poppy. You have a lot to learn. Yes, he's a prince, but you don't want that lifestyle. There are rumors…" she let the thought trail off.

I crossed my arms over my chest. I couldn't believe this was happening. My mother walked into the kitchen. My father looked out the window, watching the rain slide down the glass.

"She's right," he said a moment later, turning from the window. "You don't want this."

If I could convince him this was a good thing, that I was happy, he could talk to my mother. I took his hands and squeezed them. "I do. There's no one else I'd rather be with. He'll take care of me…of us."

My father's eyes met mine. He squeezed my hands but said nothing. Another tear slid down my cheek and I pulled my hand away. The kitchen door swung open, and my mother rejoined us. She tossed a bag to the floor.

"We don't have much time," she said. "Pack a few things. Just the necessities."

My hands flew to my hips. "I'm not leaving."

My mother stepped closer, taking my hands in hers. "Yes, you are. We all are. We've been wanting to leave for a while. Now's the perfect time."

I shook my head. Anger raced through me. I couldn't believe they were doing this. I had to talk to Thaniel.

She gripped my arms. I struggled, trying to break free. I needed to buy some time. They would come to see this was a good thing.

My mother dropped my right arm to reach into her pocket. I used the moment to free my left arm from her tight grip. I stumbled backward as she withdrew a small glass bottle etched with thin green lines. She unscrewed the top and tipped it over her palm.

Before I could register what was happening, she blew the pale-brown powder at me. I turned, but wasn't fast enough. The powder landed on my skin.

My eyes met hers one last time before my legs gave out and I fell to the floor.

POPPY

When I opened my eyes, darkness greeted me. The room was silent as I unpacked the latest memory. A part of me couldn't believe my parents had lied to me for so long. They hadn't even let me see Thaniel after the decree.

Another part of me wasn't as surprised. All the signs were there. I had just been too naïve to pick up on them.

Looking back on my last night in White Bridge gave me a new perspective. When I met my parents in the driveway, they had almost seemed to expect it. Almost as if they had been waiting for Thaniel to find us all along.

I sat up, straining my eyes in the dark. Was he still in the room with me?

When we arrived at the inn, he insisted on sleeping in my room. It hadn't bothered me; I couldn't shake the magmar's warning. He had taken the small couch, leaving me the bed. In the morning, we would meet up with the others and make our way to Greymoore Manor. At the edge of the bed, the dog slept, curled at my feet. He had followed us, and both Thaniel and Cerros reluctantly agreed to let him stay.

I rubbed my forehead, trying to push the latest memory away. My stomach coiled; I didn't enjoy knowing there was a whole other side of me I didn't even know. As the magic binding my memories dissipated, would I even recognize myself?

I threw the blankets off. When my feet touched the ground, I was surprised at how cold it was. When Thaniel didn't move, I carefully made my way to the glass door that led to the small balcony.

Gray clouds covered the moon, its rays struggling to peek through the darkness. I walked to the edge of the balcony, resting my arms on the railing. In the distance, the faint sound of a waterfall calmed my nerves. The air was warm, and I inhaled deeply, enjoying the moment of solitude.

When I was with Thaniel, the more I remembered about my past, the angrier I became with my parents. I thought our relationship had been stronger. I never thought they had been lying to me.

I still didn't understand why they had such an aversion to him. Sure, he was Shadow Marked, but when they knew him, he had only been a teenager. Before they took me to White Bridge, I had been excited about the possibility of a future with him. I had been excited that we were fated. He cared about me, and I felt safe with him. Did I want to leave?

"Are you okay?"

I turned at Thaniel's voice. He was leaning against the door frame. His hair was tousled from sleep. My eyes fell to his chiseled abs, and my skin grew warm.

"I'm fine," I answered.

I turned my back to him, resting against the railing once more. Without a shirt, he was too distracting. I needed to clear my head and focus on one thing at a time. I couldn't let him distract me. I had to work out my feelings on my own.

He didn't take the hint. A moment later, he was next to me,

looking off into the distance. His shoulder brushed mine, and I trembled at the touch.

"Did you sleep okay?" he asked, his voice raspy.

I nodded. "Another memory came back."

He turned to face me. "A good one, I hope."

My eyes met his. The air around us seemed to pulse. I suppressed the urge to reach out and run my hand along his bare chest. Finally, my brain registered that I should answer.

"My birthday dress," I began, my voice cracking. "Did you buy it for me?"

He looked away, past the railing again. Even though he didn't have to answer—I already knew the truth—I wanted to hear it from him. My parents wouldn't have been able to afford the dress on their own. Why hadn't they told me?

"I did," he answered after an uncomfortable moment of silence. "I had our seamstress make it. You wanted a new dress. I knew your parents wouldn't have been able to buy you one. I only wanted to help."

What else had my parents kept from me? My stomach sank when I remembered my father's job at the castle. Had Thaniel been responsible for that?

The air continued to crackle, reminding me of the moments before a thunderstorm. George had never made me feel this way. There was something between us, something I desperately wanted to explore.

"I've liked you since the moment I met you." He held my gaze. "You didn't treat me as a prince. I was just Thaniel. I could be myself with you. Even if the decree hadn't happened, I was still going to choose you. It will always be you."

My eyes widened. Was that even possible? Would his family have let him be with me if the decree hadn't happened? If we hadn't been fated, there would always be the possibility that he would find his soulmate. Would I have taken the chance?

I realized it didn't matter. We were fated. He was mine. I smiled as a warmth spread through my chest.

Thaniel placed his finger underneath my chin, gently lifting my face. "Poppy, I don't think I can let you go."

I held my breath. I couldn't move even if I wanted. His touch sent a shiver through me. At that moment, I knew I couldn't leave him, not yet. I owed it to myself to explore our connection.

"I don't think I want you to let me go."

His lips parted, and his breath quickened. I stepped closer, and he wrapped his arms around me, pulling me toward him. I placed my hand on his chest and looked into his eyes. He smiled and my heart raced. My mind cleared, imagining what our future would hold.

He lowered his head and placed his lips on mine. I leaned into his kiss. For a moment, my world crumbled, one layer at a time, leaving nothing but us.

His hands moved to my back, and he picked me up, somehow bringing me even closer. I wrapped my legs around his waist as he carried me toward the door. My lips searched his, exploring them as if it was my first kiss. He groaned softly and a fire in my belly ignited. I wanted him more than I had ever wanted anyone. His touch awakened me.

When my back met the hard wall, I closed my eyes and brought my hands around his neck, running my fingers through his hair. A loud sigh escaped his lips, and he placed his head on my forehead. I used the opportunity to catch my breath and reground myself to his touch. A part of me wondered if I was dreaming.

"I'll follow you anywhere," he whispered, his voice electrifying my nerves. "If you want to go back to White Bridge, I'll go with you."

I placed my hands on his chest, my fingers running over his smooth skin. All the tension left me. This was what I had wanted. A chance to explore our connection. I wasn't sure I was ready to leave White Bridge, but he was willing to leave his family, his life, to come with me. My stomach sank when I realized what he would be giving up. "You're a prince. You can't just leave."

He pulled away, his eyes meeting mine. "I'd do anything for you."

I looked away, guilt gnawing at me. Did I even want to go back to White Bridge? Was I going to finish the semester after everything I had been through?

He placed his hand under my chin, gently guiding me to him. "Cerros is next in line. No one will care if I'm gone. I can always come back when I need to."

"We have time," I said. "Let's not rush anything."

He nodded. "You should go to sleep. We have a few hours before we're meeting everyone."

He gently lowered me to the floor. I followed him inside, my legs weak. He closed the door to the balcony, and I climbed into bed. I pulled the blankets up to my chin, my heart beating a mile a minute as my emotions ran wild. Excitement, nervousness, and fear all washed over me. Would I even be able to sleep?

A loud crash echoed from the hall. I stood from the bed as the front door burst open, the wood splintering from the hinges. A man in a dark brown cloak, his hood covering his head, stepped into the room.

We didn't have time to move before two more people appeared, blocking our escape.

THANIEL

As the door splintered off the hinges, my eyes snapped to Poppy. Who were these people? Where was Cerros?

I scanned the room, searching for an escape. Unfortunately, the only real entrance was the front door. We were on the second floor, the balcony high above the ground.

The man in the brown cloak stepped forward. He removed his hood, and my jaw slackened. Cullen's eyes met mine, and a dark smile spread across his lips.

"What's the meaning of this?" I growled. "Cullen, what're you doing?"

He gestured the others into the room. He clicked his tongue before pulling up his sleeve, revealing a large, thick scar that ran from the back of his elbow to his wrist. "You don't remember this, do you?"

My mind raced. I had trusted him. Was he working for Enley? Did he know where Poppy's parents were the whole time? Had he poisoned Thea? The dog growled and Poppy ran to him.

"I'm not sure what a scar has to do with your betrayal."

Cullen's lips twisted in a grimace. When he looked up again, his eyes danced with a rage all their own. My marks vibrated, the tattoos thrumming to life. There was more to our curse that I wasn't yet willing to share. I suspected Poppy's parents had heard the rumors, and that's why they had taken her. I couldn't be sure, but it didn't matter.

The truth was, I craved the kills.

"I got these scars saving you the night your curse was triggered. I thought you were my friend." His eyes narrowed at Poppy before turning to his accomplices. "Take her."

I balled my fists; the adrenaline spiking through me. "No one touches her."

Cullen's lips curled. "We don't need to touch her to kill her."

I stepped forward. "I trusted you. All this time—"

"I trusted you once," Cullen snapped, his words clipped. "I trusted your family. Until you killed Alora."

I looked into the hallway, hoping Cerros would hear. He should be in his room next door. I needed his help. I could take out Cullen, but I didn't think I could take out all three at once. I had to keep him talking. I had to bide our time and hope Cerros was close.

"Alora?" I asked.

Cullen rolled his sleeve down, recovering the scar. "My girlfriend Alora, but of course, you don't remember that. You've been too consumed with finding *her*."

The hair on my arms prickled. Alora. My father's cook? She worked for us two years ago. She only lasted a year before she tried to poison my father. I didn't even know they had been dating. The marks on my chest electrified.

"We were going to get married," he said. "Until you killed her."

Poppy gasped. I ran my tongue over my lips, remembering the night clearly. The mark I received from killing her grew hot, my skin yearning for more.

Cullen's eyes traveled to Poppy. "He didn't tell you one of

those marks"—he gestured angrily at my chest— "was for killing my girlfriend, did he?"

"No," she whispered over the dog's bark. "He wouldn't..."

I couldn't listen to her defend me. I wasn't who she thought I was. When she left five years ago, I hadn't triggered my curse.

"I did." I turned to her. "I would do it again. She tried to kill my father. She was working for Enley." I turned back to Cullen. "I didn't even know you were dating."

"I guess it doesn't matter," Cullen said.

The man to my right stepped forward. I followed his movement, unwilling to let him any closer. I reached into my pocket, withdrawing my knife. I didn't think I would need it; I could kill him with my bare hands, but I was hoping to pass it to Poppy if given the chance.

"You've taken a vow to protect my family," I said. "She tried to kill your king."

"There's something unnatural about you," Cullen said. "Your marks—they're trophies, highlighting the lives you've taken. When you activated the curse, I knew it wasn't right. Alora brought me to Enley. They were cousins. I bet you didn't know that."

I didn't care they were cousins. After I killed Alora, I hadn't thought of her again. When I killed Cullen, I wouldn't think of him again.

This was why I didn't have friends.

Where were the other soldiers Cerros had procured? Where was Lucien? My father had sent him to scout Greymoore Manor yesterday. He was supposed to meet us here.

"You tried poisoning me," Poppy spoke up. "It was you? Why?"

I nearly dropped my knife. The rage inside me boiled. My marks burned. Cullen was the reason Thea was sick. Her still body, pale face, and labored breathing all came to mind. Cullen had nearly killed her, had tried to kill my fated. My muscles tensed, my fingers gripping the metal hilt tightly.

"Too bad Thea took the brunt of it," Cullen said. "It was the perfect plan. A lot of thought went into that."

"Why?" Poppy's voice cracked. "I haven't done anything to you."

Cullen exhaled loudly. "Revenge mainly. Enley's paying me quite well, that helps."

This wasn't the same Cullen I knew. Standing before me was a stranger. How had he fooled me? Suddenly, everything clicked into place. Cullen had told Enley where Poppy lived. He had followed me; he knew when I left the castle. I ran my finger over the blade when a younger man ran into the room.

Cullen's face twisted in anger. "You're supposed to be our lookout."

I used the opportunity to turn to Poppy. She was holding the damn dog. I tossed her the knife. It landed on the bed next to her. She looked up, her eyes wide. I turned back, only to find one of Cullen's accomplices. He swung his arm, but I ducked. The man lost his balance, and I used the opportunity to tackle him. I wrapped my arms around him, pushing him toward the wall.

"I see I'm just in time."

I turned at the voice. Cerros.

Cullen's face twisted in anger as my brother stepped into the room slowly. He hadn't made it far when another imposing figure, clad in black armor, appeared from the shadows. Lucien's eyes swept over the scene before him. He pulled a large silver sword from the sheath at his side.

At my distraction, the man broke free. I stumbled backward, tripping over Poppy's bag. The man ran toward me, his knife poised to strike. I rolled to my right, using my leg to trip him. At the door, Cerros and Cullen were fighting.

"Thaniel," Poppy screamed. "Look out!"

I turned, only to come face-to-face with Cullen's other accomplice. His hands raised; a large knife aimed at me. Before I could react, the man stopped, his eyes wide. Bright red blood poured out of his mouth, cascading down his lips. He coughed, and more blood spilled down his chin. His eyes dulled and his jaw slackened before he toppled to the floor. Standing behind him was Lucien. In his hands was the bloody sword ripped from the man's back.

POPPY

The man in black, death personified, wiped the blade of his sword on the dead man at his feet. The room spun. I froze. I couldn't make sense of what was happening around me.

The dog jumped from my lap. He landed on the floor, barking wildly at the commotion. I looked up just in time to see Cullen slash Cerros with his knife. Cerros stepped backward before falling to his knees. Thaniel and the man in black were fighting Cullen's other accomplice.

My eyes scanned the room, finally spotting the younger man that had run in before Cerros. He was against the far wall, his eyes wide. Cullen turned, a smile parting his lips when he saw me.

Thaniel spun around, leaving the man in black armor. He ran to Cullen, clutching his cloak. I realized my only escape was the balcony. I ran to the door, the dog at my heels.

"Don't let her escape!" Cullen cried.

I looked back. The young man was still across the room. When he didn't make a move to attack, I pulled the door open and ran onto the balcony.

Flashes of my kiss with Thaniel overtook me. How had the night taken such a turn? He ignited something inside me. I couldn't leave him. Where was I even going to go? Would I survive the jump?

I placed my hands on the railing and looked down. It was too dark to see how far the jump would be. The dog pushed his way between my feet. I picked him up, stroking his nose.

A sharp gust of wind sent a shiver down my spine. I was in way over my head. I had been living in a fantasy world. How did I think I could save my parents and Addie? I froze at the mere presence of danger.

Heavy footfalls sounded behind me. The man in black stepped onto the balcony. His hand fell to his side, the tip of the sword resting on the ground.

His gray eyes swept across the balcony. "You shouldn't be out here alone."

My body trembled. The dog jumped out of my grip, running toward the man. Suddenly, Thaniel ran out. He wrapped me in his arms, hugging me tightly. I relaxed in his embrace. Now that I was safe in his arms, the tears came. He pulled me even closer, his fingers stroking my hair.

"Where is he?" I asked. "Is Cerros—"

"I'm fine," Cerros answered from the doorway. "Thanks to Lucien."

I pulled away from Thaniel, and that's when I saw the blood on his clothes. "Are you okay?"

He nodded. "Most of this isn't even mine."

My eyes flew to his chest, searching for any other marks. If anything, I was only curious. I was just so grateful he was here with me.

"I didn't kill anyone," he said. "Lucien got them all."

With his sword, Lucien traced an X onto the floor of the balcony. I wanted to ask why, but the words didn't come. Something about him scared me. He didn't seem real. Even his all-black armor was imposing. In one swift move, he swung his sword up, resting it on his shoulder. For a moment, I wondered if he was Shadow Marked. I couldn't see any tattoos; his armor covered his skin completely.

"You're lucky I was here." Lucien stepped forward. "What are we going to do with the last?"

"He could be useful," Cerros said. "It was smart to spare him."

I had almost forgotten the young man that had come in prior to Cerros. During the fighting, he had stayed near the wall. Did he know where my parents and Addie were? I stepped away from Thaniel, toward the door, but he stopped me.

"You don't want to go in there."

I froze. Lucien had killed three people. Their bodies were inside our room. Even though they were going to kill me, it still felt wrong.

"I'll get him," Lucien said, his voice flat. "He's tied to the door."

I looked up, my eyes meeting Thaniel's. He took my hands, weaving his fingers in mine. I clung to him tightly as Lucien led out his prisoner. My stomach churned. Now that the threat had passed, I recognized him.

Standing before me was Addie's crush from McLaughlin's.

*L*ucien led the man forward. His hands were bound behind his back. Dirt, sweat, and blood covered his face, but I still recognized him. He was the last person to see Addie. What had he done with her? Rage boiled inside me.

"Where is she?" I screamed. "What did you do to her? To my parents?" I balled my hands into fists. I needed them to be okay. If he had done something to them…I couldn't even finish the thought. I stepped forward, but Thaniel held me back.

"Do you know him?"

My jaw clenched. "He was the last person to see Addie before she disappeared at McLaughlin's."

Everything unraveled. I couldn't take it anymore. Nothing was even making sense. What were the odds that Addie would have met someone from this land? He had to be working for Enley.

"Addie had been dancing with him," I added. "We had seen him around the club before."

Lucien tightened his grip on the stranger. He flinched but said nothing. His silence angered me even more.

"What did you do to them?" Thaniel asked.

When the man didn't answer, Cerros stepped forward. He stood directly in front of him, an arm's length from Lucien. "What's your name?"

The man's lower lip trembled, but he remained silent.

I clenched my fists even tighter. I had to remain calm. This man was the key to finding my parents and Addie. I was so close to finding them.

"We can do this the easy way, or the hard way," Lucien said. "That choice is up to you."

Cerros cleared his throat. "It didn't seem as if you were voluntarily working with Enley. You didn't want to fight. That's why we spared you."

"I didn't," the man finally said, his voice a whisper. "They have someone I love."

I looked at Thaniel. Could we trust anything he said? Even though he hadn't seemed to want to fight, he had been with Enley.

"He has someone you love?" Thaniel asked.

The man nodded. "I don't care what you do to me. I'll never be free. When he finds out I did nothing back there, that I didn't help..." He looked at me, his eyes watering. "I'm a dead man anyway."

"I asked you your name," Cerros said. "What is it?"

I wanted to scream. Why was Cerros obsessed with his name? I just needed him to talk. I didn't care what his name was. I didn't even care what happened to him afterward.

"Marcus," the man answered. "My name's Marcus."

"You must know who we are," Cerros said.

Marcus shook his head before pointing at me. "I only know her."

My stomach churned. He knew who I was, and I knew nothing about him. Had he danced with Addie to get close to me? Had he planned on taking her that night? I wanted to scream, to yell at him, to force him to tell me everything.

Thaniel placed his hand on my arm. He leaned close, whispering in my ear, "Let Cerros handle it. He'll get him to talk."

I bit the inside of my cheeks, forcing myself to remain calm. Marcus shifted on his feet, his eyes on me. My hands trembled when I remembered he had been in my Shakespeare class. When I heard my name, he had been behind me. Had he been messing with me? How long had he been watching me?

"I'm Prince Cerros Ashton-Dumont from Marwood." Cerros pointed to Thaniel. "This is Prince Thaniel Ashton-Dumont." He then gestured to the man holding him. "This is Lucien Astor, the king's private mercenary. Let's just say you don't want to get on his bad side."

As if to prove the point, Lucien said, "I did just kill three people."

Marcus looked away. His lower lip quivered, but beyond that he appeared calm. My nerves were tight, wound beyond anything I had ever experienced. Cullen's betrayal stung, and I had barely known him. The attack had put the situation into perspective. I couldn't do this on my own. I needed to be patient, to let them get the answers.

"Start from the beginning," Thaniel said. "How did you get caught up with Enley?"

Marcus looked up, his eyes meeting Thaniel's. "He has my brother. He promised that if I did what he asked, he'd let him go. That was three months ago."

I swallowed, pushing the anger down. If he was telling the truth, he was doing everything for someone he loved. I was doing the same. I couldn't blame him.

"I've seen you before Friday," I said. "You've been at McLaughlin's a few times. You were in my Shakespeare class. Was it all part of the plan?"

His eyes met mine again. "He sent me there. You were hard to get close to. You were all over your boyfriend."

Next to me, Thaniel stiffened. I knew he didn't like to think about George. Even after our moment on the balcony, it had been a painful reminder of our time apart.

"I was the backup plan that night," Marcus continued. "Addie was an easy way to get to your parents."

"Backup?" I asked. "What does that mean?" As soon as the words were out of my mouth, his statement made sense. I had been attacked the night Addie was taken. "Never mind."

Thaniel exhaled loudly. I reached for him, twining my fingers through his again. He squeezed my hand tightly.

I turned to Marcus. "I just want my family back. You know what it feels like."

He was silent. I held my breath, waiting for his answer.

"Tell me about your brother," Cerros said.

Marcus bit his lip, a tear sliding down his cheek. "He's only twelve. I didn't mean for any of this to happen." He looked at me. "I'm sorry. I shouldn't have done it. I shouldn't have helped him."

"Was Enley there? In McLaughlin's?" I asked.

"He was in White Bridge," he answered. "He wasn't at the bar. I took Addie, I tricked her. She thought we were only going outside for some air. I drove her to Enley, and we took your parents."

I swallowed. I didn't understand why Enley would even take my parents. Why didn't he try to take me at McLaughlin's? Why was he banking on other people taking me out? Why did he rely on others to do his dirty work?

"Where are they?" I asked. "I need to know if they're okay. When was the last time you saw them? What did Enley say he was going to do with them?"

Marcus hesitated, as if forming the words to answer.

"They're with my brother, imprisoned in Greymoore Manor. He knows you'll come for them."

A twinge of excitement ran through me. They were alive, and now I knew where they were.

"Then I guess you're taking us to Greymoore Manor," Thaniel said.

"No," Marcus said. "I can't, he'll kill me."

Lucien raised the sword. "I'll kill you."

Cerros held up his hand, gesturing Lucien to back away before turning to Marcus. "If you help us, if you get us inside Greymoore Manor, we'll help rescue your brother."

My excitement was short-lived. We needed to save my family. We wouldn't have time to save Marcus's brother, too.

As soon as the thoughts washed over me, I knew I had to rein them in. Marcus missed his brother just as much as I missed my family. His role in their abduction didn't escape me, but I would have done the same thing in his situation.

"I'm not promising anything," Thaniel said. "My priority is Poppy and her family."

Marcus nodded. "They're in the same place. They're in the basement. Enley keeps all his prisoners heavily guarded."

Lucien smiled. "I'm in for a fight."

I looked up at Thaniel. Maybe this was it. Maybe we could rescue my family after all. Maybe there was an end to the nightmare that had consumed my life.

He frowned. "Poppy, when we go back inside, don't look."

Lucien chuckled. "I had a little too much fun."

THANIEL

$\mathcal{I}$ ushered Poppy through the room quickly. The coppery smell of blood hit my nose, and I balked for only a moment. She picked up her pace, the dog squirming in her hands. I didn't know what we were going to do with it. We couldn't take it with us to Greymoore Manor.

My eyes caught sight of Cullen's lifeless body. His betrayal stung. I thought we were friends. I didn't know he had been dating Alora, no idea he had been plotting against my family. While he had shielded me that day four years ago, my curse had been stronger. He said it best—there was something unnatural about me.

Behind us, Lucien led Marcus, and Cerros brought up the rear. I wasn't sure if we should trust Marcus. He had been responsible for taking Addie. A part of me was angry with myself that I hadn't caught on sooner. I should have picked up that he hadn't been from White Bridge, that he had been watching Poppy and her friend.

I was losing my touch.

When we were in the hallway, I pointed to the right, toward the stairs. The dog barked once when someone opened their door to peek out. When they saw us, the door quickly shut again. Although the hall was dark, shadows crept up the wall, silently watching.

We found Bran at the long bar, sipping a drink. Even though I had known him my entire life, I didn't trust him. He had owned the inn for years; he inherited it when his uncle had passed. I directed Poppy to a chair and sat next to him, signaling to the man behind the bar for a drink.

Bran set his glass down. "I've had a few noise complaints from your room. Are you settled in for the night?"

I bit my tongue to keep from striking him. He knew what was happening and did nothing to help. The man behind the bar set a crystal glass of whiskey in front of me and moved to Poppy. I heard her ask for water before I turned back to Bran.

"The drinks are on the house," I stated. "We'll need two more, for Cerros and Lucien."

Bran turned in his seat. "The young man?"

Somehow, I had forgotten about Marcus. I picked up the glass in front of me. The whiskey burned the entire way down, warming my throat. Bran didn't like to spend his money on the good stuff. Instead, he stocked the bar with cheap vintages, knowing they would sell out of necessity. He liked to cut corners; turn the other way if there was a benefit to him.

I set the glass down. "Nothing for him. I need to know if Cullen said anything to you before coming up."

He wrapped his fingers around his glass. The man behind the bar set a water in front of Poppy. Cerros made his way to the opposite side of Bran.

"They only asked what room you were in," he finally answered. "I knew you would be fine; I saw Lucien arrive a few minutes before."

My marks tingled, a sign of my anger. "There's quite the mess in our room. I expect you'll take care of it before we return."

Bran took another slow sip of his drink. I stood, waiting as Cerros and Lucien downed theirs. Poppy had already finished her water and was now scratching the dog behind the ears.

I turned to Bran once more. "And I expect the dog will be taken care of while we're gone."

POPPY

I was over walking. I missed my car, and I could only imagine the number of miles we had racked up in the last two days. I never wanted to walk anywhere again.

My stomach rumbled. Cerros had bought banana and poppy seed muffins from Bran before we left. While they had been delicious, they hadn't been enough to fill me. I longed for my father's cheeseburgers; the gooey cheese melted into the toasted bun called to me. I licked my lips, as if that would satiate my craving.

Marcus led us through the forest in silence. He had wanted to avoid the main roads as it would just increase the chances Enley, or one of his followers, would see us. At the moment, the only thing we had going for us was the element of surprise.

A loud crack of thunder echoed around us. My heart raced a mile a minute. It instantly brought me back to the inn, to the moment the door cracked off its hinges. I didn't think I would ever forget the sound.

Drizzling rain fell around us, as sparks of lightning lit the way. The only thing that kept me going was the thought that I would soon see my parents and Addie.

Marcus stopped walking. "It's through these trees."

"What's the plan?" Thaniel asked. "How are we going to get in?"

"There's an old stable in the backyard," he answered. "There's a passage that goes to the basement, to the root cellar."

I looked at Thaniel. Could it be that easy? He kept his gaze forward, as if searching the tree line before us.

Cerros waved his arm. "Lead the way."

Marcus paused. For a moment, I feared he would rescind his offer to help. The rain intensified, and I stepped toward a tree, finding shelter under the branches.

Thaniel turned to me. "Maybe you should stay."

I shook my head. He couldn't be serious. There was no way I would stay behind. Besides, would I be any safer by myself? I pushed forward, away from the tree.

"No." I didn't even wait for his agreement. I made my way to Marcus, standing beside him. "Well, what are we waiting for? Let's go."

Marcus didn't miss a beat. He walked toward the line of trees, their branches seeming to reach for us. Thaniel pushed his way toward me, leaving Cerros and Lucien to bring up the rear. I walked through a thick spiderweb. My skin tingled as I imagined what kind of spider had been lying in wait.

Before us, Greymoore Manor appeared. Through the light of the moon, it looked imposing, menacing, even. It was built of dark stone, and green ivy snaked its way up to the roof, entwining the large chimney. Soft yellow light poured through the small windows on either end of the second floor, like two beady yellow eyes watching us. Standing near the front door were two guards.

Marcus gestured to our left. The ice-cold raindrops echoed as they hit the leaves, creating a symphony that served as the soundtrack of our journey. I focused on the sound, using it as a distraction from my thoughts. We were so close to my parents; I could almost feel them. Even though I was nervous, a thrill of excitement washed over me.

Tiny pinpricks made their way up my arm, and I looked down just in time to see a dime-sized black fly. I shook my arm, and it flew toward the manor. I strained my ears, listening for any sign the guards had seen us. All that met me was the rain.

High above, something screeched. I jumped, my heart beating so fast it hurt to breathe. My hand flew to my chest, as if my touch would calm my racing nerves. Thaniel narrowed his eyes at me, and I realized it was only an animal. While I wasn't sure what it was, no one else had been fazed. That was a good sign, right?

Thankfully, no one had been guarding the stables, and we could sneak inside easily. Although it was dark, a soft light lit up the room, revealing large stalls with hay covering the floor. Marcus led us to the last stall on the right. He lifted the latch and swung the door in. A horse neighed, filling the silence.

"Where's the entrance?" Thaniel growled.

Marcus stepped toward the horse to rub its nose. He kicked at the hay on the floor, pushing it aside with his shoe. The horse bent down to retrieve some of the hay, chewing it loudly. When the outline of a door appeared, Marcus knelt, using his hands to uncover the passage.

"That leads inside?" Cerros asked. "It's not locked?"

Marcus placed his fingers on the ridge. "I think it's mostly forgotten. I found it by chance, cleaning Midnight's stall. Another one of my prison sentences. I never told anyone."

The horse neighed when it heard its name. Marcus pulled open the heavy door, setting it on the ground. I stepped closer, looking into the hole. The passage was dark and dusty, thick cobwebs flanked the opening. A set of rough, wooden stairs descended, disappearing into the abyss.

Marcus ran a hand through his brown hair, pushing it away from his eyes. "I'll lead the way."

"I'll go next," Lucien said, pushing his way forward. "Just in case."

The hair on my arms stood on end and I rubbed my hands down them, using the friction to warm me. When Lucien disappeared, Cerros peered into the hole. He looked at Thaniel.

"Ready brother?"

Thaniel nodded. "I'll go, then Poppy."

Cerros nodded his agreement. Thaniel pulled me close, kissing my forehead. When he pulled away, he stepped into the hole. Midnight gave one last neigh before turning away. The adrenaline coursing through me made me dizzy, threatening my balance. I placed my foot on the first step and crept down. More than once, Cerros ran into me.

"The stairs end here," Marcus called. "It gets tight."

As I descended the last few steps, I noticed the walls closing in; the walkway narrowing. The ceiling seemed to drop, and my breathing increased. I didn't like enclosed spaces, and the walkway was tiny, with just enough room to walk upright, single file.

Dust filled the air, kicked up from our passing feet. I ran into too many cobwebs to count. Eventually, the ceiling dropped too far for us to walk upright. I crawled on my hands and knees, my fingers digging into the caked, dry dirt.

Up ahead, a crack of light appeared. Marcus had opened a door. He slid out of the passage, Lucien right behind him. I steadied my breathing, my ears strained for any indication they had been seen. I didn't even think that we could turn around if they had been caught. It was too tight to do anything except push forward.

When Thaniel crawled out of the passage, I paused. A moment later, he gestured it was safe to join him. As excitement washed over me, I crawled through the door.

Besides us, the room was empty. The floor was packed dirt and there was only one small window on the opposite wall. My hand trembled as I brushed off my clothes. Cerros stepped out after me.

The door we had crawled out of was made of wood. A rusted iron handle had originally locked it in place, but it appeared broke.

"They should be just down the hall," Marcus said. "I held up my end of the deal. Don't forget about my brother."

A pit formed in my stomach. This seemed too easy. Not only were we able to get inside the stables, but the manor itself, without being seen. It all felt too convenient. Could it possibly be this easy to rescue my parents and Addie? If so, why hadn't they escaped?

My knees buckled as I looked up at Thaniel, trying to gauge if my relief would be short-lived. He stepped closer to me, his eyes never leaving the door. I strained my ears, listening for any sign that we were heading into a trap. All I heard was Thaniel's shallow breathing.

Lucien withdrew his sword. Marcus opened the door slowly.

I let out the breath I had been holding when silence met us. There were no guards, no one waiting for us. Marcus and Lucien slipped into the hall. Thaniel took my hand, and I held him back.

"Doesn't this seem a little too easy?" my voice cracked. "Something feels off."

Thaniel looked at Cerros, a silent conversation passing between them. I bit my lip, waiting for them to include me.

"You can stay here," Cerros finally said. "If something happens, if we're not back in a few minutes, make your way out of the tunnel."

I sighed. "And then what? I don't know the area at all."

Lucien appeared at the door. His brow furrowed as he looked from Thaniel to Cerros. "The coast is clear. The room they're being held in is right next door. We have to move."

Thaniel looked back at me. "I'm not leaving you. If you stay, I stay."

I was so close to ending the nightmare. I couldn't let my fear get in the way. If they weren't being guarded, now was our chance. "Let's go," I said before I lost my nerve.

We made our way into the hall. Marcus was nowhere to be seen. My stomach sank, my nerves on fire.

Lucien stopped at the open door to his right, his sword poised. When he disappeared inside the room, my legs grew weak. Thaniel and Cerros stepped close to me, holding knives in front of them. I reached inside my pocket and withdrew my knife, the one that Thaniel had thrown me when Cullen attacked.

The hall was quiet. It seemed as if no one was in the basement. Where was everyone? Where had Marcus gone? Our wait seemed to stretch. Seconds turned to minutes and just when I thought I couldn't take it anymore, Lucien waved us in.

When I stepped inside the room, I hadn't been prepared for what I saw. It was larger than the room we had left, but had the same dirt floor. There were no windows, only a small light near the far corner. Dividing the room was a long row of silver bars. My jaw slackened. My parents and Addie were on the other side. Their faces were dirty, and their clothes were torn, but they were alive.

"Pop?" my father called, finally noticing me.

I ran to the metal bars, sticking my arm in to reach my father. He scrambled to meet me, taking my hand and bringing it to his cheek. Beside him, my mother and Addie appeared. Tears streamed down my face. I had so many questions, so many things I wanted to tell them, but we didn't have time. We had to leave before anyone found us.

"Where's the door?" I asked, my eyes scanning the metal bars. "How did you get in here?"

"Poppy," my mother said. "Go. They'll be back any minute."

I shook my head. Did she really think I could leave them? I hadn't come this far to give up. I took my father's hands and set the knife in his palm. They needed it more than I did. I had Thaniel.

"The door's here," Thaniel called.

I turned at the sound of his voice. He was near the far wall, pulling at the bars. Lucien joined him, his sword raised.

"Welcome," a voice called. "You made this too easy."

POPPY

An arrow flew past me, barely missing my ear. I dropped my father's hand to turn around. Standing at the door was a tall, skinny man. His long black hair hung loosely down his back. His eyes scanned the room, finally resting on me. He smiled before raising the bow again, setting the arrow and pulling it into position.

"Poppy, move!" Thaniel called, running to me.

I froze. The man released the arrow. Behind me, someone screamed, but I couldn't make sense of the words. At that moment, time slowed. I couldn't move even if I wanted. The arrow shot forward when Thaniel pushed into me, sending me to the floor.

I landed on my arm, and shockwaves of pain radiated through me. Thaniel fell next to me, a long arrow protruding from his shoulder. I sat just in time to see more people appear at the door.

"You couldn't resist, could you?" the man said, looking at Thaniel. "The curse is always there, always in the background."

Thaniel sat. "What do you know about our curse, Enley?"

My stomach dropped. This was the man who abducted my

parents and Addie. He had forced them here, against their will, and locked them up, kept them as prisoners. I clenched my fists, digging my fingers into the dirt floor.

Enley dropped his hands, tossing the bow to the ground. "I know having a fated is the biggest weakness there is. How can you be strong when you're constantly worried about someone else? It's a small price to pay for stealing the throne."

Lucien stepped forward; his sword raised. Thaniel held his arm up and he stopped. I pushed myself backward, toward the cell housing my parents and Addie. It didn't escape me that Marcus had been lying. There had been no one else imprisoned with them.

Thaniel stood, the arrow still in his shoulder. "Let Poppy and her family go. They have nothing to do with this."

"Don't they?" Enley asked. "They're the easiest way to you. And look at my luck, not one but two princes of Marwood."

The sound of shuffling met my ears. I turned to find my father pressed against the bars.

His breathing was labored as he whispered, "You have to leave. Don't worry about your mom and me."

I shook my head. How could he say that? Did he honestly think I could leave them? My mother nodded. I searched for Addie, the dim light making it hard to see. She was against the far wall. When our eyes met, the tears came.

My body trembled. I had come all this way. We had almost rescued them. I knew we shouldn't have trusted Marcus. I dug my fingers into the hard dirt again, prying it apart, before turning back to Enley.

"What do you think is going to happen when you kill us?" I spat. "Do you think you'll be welcomed in Marwood? Do you think you'll somehow be king?"

Enley set his stony stare on me. His nostrils flared and his lips curved into a wicked smile. "That's only the beginning.

Soon, the Ashton-Dumonts will be no more. It'll be easy to step in, the grandson of the true king, the line restored."

I ground my fingers deeper into the dirt, using it as a distraction. The room was hot and muggy. My thoughts jumbled. Beside me, Thaniel gripped the arrow and pulled it out smoothly. A low groan escaped his lips.

Across the room, Cerros made a move toward his brother, but Lucien held him back. He whispered something, but I was too far away to hear. I only hoped he had a plan. Cerros narrowed his eyes, leaning closer to Lucien as if he couldn't hear. I had to create a distraction; keep Enley talking. Maybe if I did, Lucien could take over.

I turned to Enley again, asking the first thing that came to mind. "Where's Marcus?"

Enley's eyes lit. "The traitor's dead, along with his brother."

My stomach sank. Had he been telling the truth the whole time? He hadn't betrayed us after all. Before I could process it, Lucien ran forward. Those behind Enley sprang into motion, pushing him back to safety.

Chaos broke loose as Thaniel and Cerros joined the fray. Before I lost my nerve, I turned toward the cell, searching for the opening. My thoughts were frantic. I couldn't think straight. Even though I was angry with my parents, I pushed forward.

"Poppy," my mother screamed, her eyes wide at the commotion. "He's behind you."

Sweat pooled at my temple. My body shook as I turned around. Enley was before me. Thaniel, Cerros, and Lucien were engaged in their own battles, and my parents and Addie couldn't help. I fell to the ground, my knees weak with fear. Enley knelt before me, wrapping his hands around my throat.

$\mathcal{E}$nley bared his teeth as he tightened his long fingers around my neck. I struggled in his grip but couldn't break free. He was strong.

Behind me, my father reached through the bars, trying to help. The knife fell and my father swore. I gasped for breath, my fingers prying at Enley. I kicked my feet wildly, frantically searching for relief.

"Just let go," Enley whispered, his eyes alight. "Stop fighting."

He was so close I smelled his breath. Cinnamon and orange surrounded me, reminding me of a fall day in White Bridge. My hands fell limp at my sides. I dug my fingers into the dirt, grasping for a weapon, anything to use against him. He couldn't win. I wasn't going without a fight.

I scooped up as much dirt as I could. When my palms were full, I brought my arms up, tossing it at his face. He startled, loosening his grip for only a moment. But that was all I needed. I scrambled away.

Enley ran his hands over his face, wiping at the dirt. "Bitch," he sputtered. "You'll pay for that."

I stood, my eyes scanning the room. There had to be something to use against him. As much as I wanted to call for Thaniel's help, he was occupied. A large man ran for him, knocking him to the ground. Behind him, Lucien swung his sword, hitting someone in a long red cloak. A strangled scream filled the room.

"Poppy!" my mother's frantic voice called. "Watch out!"

I turned just in time to see Enley. He ran toward me, his eyes narrowed. I jumped to my right. My ankle caught the corner of a large cinderblock, and I stumbled forward. Pain radiated up my hands when I landed on them. A startled scream escaped my lips.

Enley stood over me, his eyes bright. He clasped his hands before him.

"Fight all you want," he said, his voice calm. "It all ends the same. You just have the misfortune of being a fated to the Ashton-Dumont line. My great-grandmother's curse is slowly weakening them."

I pushed myself backward. The fighting behind us was so loud I couldn't think. I only knew I had to keep him talking. I wasn't strong enough to overpower him. I had to bide my time until Thaniel could help.

My voice trembled, "Your great-grandmother started the curse?"

His head tilted, as if in thought. "Do you know how many of my people, my family, they slaughtered?" He paused. "Of course, you don't. You hardly remember Thaniel as it is."

Behind Enley, my parents were at the bars, watching. My pulse quickened, my muscles tense. Their betrayal stung. But the more I thought about it, the more I learned of life in Marwood and the Ashton-Dumont line, the more I understood their reasoning. I didn't know if I could ever forgive them, but deep down; I realized they acted on the information they had.

"I'm doing you a favor," he continued spitefully. "A life with them is a slow death anyway."

I swallowed, attempting to push the fear down. "Thaniel didn't do anything to you. You're taking your anger out on the wrong people."

A spine-chilling scream erupted behind me. I didn't turn around for fear of what I would find. Why wasn't Thaniel helping me? Was he okay?

Enley's eyes darted through the room, taking stock of the action behind me. He inhaled deeply before looking down at me again. "Do you know the field of flowers outside the castle in Marwood?" He didn't wait for me to acknowledge his question, continuing, "Every flower is a life lost. When my great-grand-mother fled, one of the few survivors, she swept her curse over the field. Each flower symbolizes one of her own. The blood-shed spilled that day. The poppy flower was our symbol, my family crest. How ironic that Thaniel's fated is named for my family's legacy."

My mind raced. Thaniel tried to burn the field of poppies and they came back. They weren't a symbol of our love that he couldn't erase. They were a symbol of his family's curse. My chest tightened when I remembered how vast the field was.

Enley looked up; his eyes wide. He turned, but Thaniel was faster. They toppled to the ground. Particles of dirt were kicked up from the impact, surrounding them. I scrambled to my feet. My heartbeat thrashed in my ears as my legs grew weak.

In one swift move, Enley tossed Thaniel off of him. He reached for the knife my father dropped. As I watched in stunned silence, he plunged it into Thaniel's arm. My stomach dropped as Thaniel cried out in pain.

All around me, everything went silent as Enley withdrew the bloody knife. He held it up, prepared to bring it down on Thaniel again. Three of Enley's army cornered Cerros and Lucien.

I had to do something; I couldn't let him win. I ran my hands down my pants, wiping the sweat from my palms. I searched the room, looking for something to use as a weapon, when I remembered the arrow. Thaniel had tossed it to the ground after pulling it from his arm. I searched for the bow. I had never used one before, but it couldn't be that hard, could it? My stomach sank. It was near the door, snapped in half. Too late, I realized it had been caught in the fighting.

Thaniel screamed again. I ran for the bloody arrow. My fingers wrapped around it, freeing it from the floor. Without thinking, I ran toward Enley. I couldn't let him hurt Thaniel, or my family.

With the strength I could muster, I pushed the tip of the arrow into his back, burying it deep in his skin. A blood-curdling scream escaped him. He turned to face me, rage dancing in his eyes.

Thaniel stood. Without missing a beat, he ran to Enley. He wrapped his arms around Enley's chest, pulling him backward. My relief was short-lived when Thaniel's eyes widened. He slammed Enley to the ground and made his way to the other side of the room. I turned; the breath caught in my throat. Cerros was on the ground, a tall man leaning over him, a long silver dagger in his hands. Lucien was near the door, fighting a man in a long black cloak.

I couldn't believe the carnage before me. Bodies littered the room; trails of blood covered the dirt floor. The smell of sweat and blood overwhelmed me. I couldn't hear anything over the thrashing of my own heartbeat in my ears. It didn't feel real.

The body closest to me had a large gash across the abdomen. A long string dangled from his pocket, a thin silver key peeking out. I froze. Could that be the key to the cell?

I scanned the room; Enley was still on the floor, in a pool of his own blood. Lucien had overtaken his opponent and was now helping Thaniel. My parents were gesturing wildly, calling for me to leave. I bent, gently pulling the string. When the key was in my hands, I ran to the cell.

"To the left," my father said. "The lock is under the bar to the left."

I froze. My muscles tensed as I watched my parents and Addie. They looked awful—deep bags lined their eyes; their clothes were dirty and torn—but they were alive, and that's all that mattered.

"Under the bar," my father rasped.

I snapped out of my thoughts. I studied the cell, finally spying the lock. It didn't escape me that even the locks were different here. Why would they be hidden?

I inserted the key. The lock popped, and the door swung open.

THANIEL

When Lucien brought the sword down, slashing the dead man at our feet, I turned, searching the room for Poppy. My muscles relaxed when I found her with her parents. Cerros stood, and I exhaled loudly, pushing away the tension.

My chest ignited, the marks buzzing with life. I had been the one to deliver the fatal blow to my brother's attacker. I wouldn't have long before a new mark appeared. But I had one more to add. I only hoped I had time before the excruciating pain overtook me.

Maybe it wouldn't be so bad. Lucien once told me each mark lessened until eventually it only felt like a scratch. I didn't know how many he had accumulated over the years; he always covered his skin.

My eyes scanned the room, looking for Enley. I was going to enjoy killing him. My shoulder screamed in agony as I made my way to where I had seen him last—where I left him unconscious. I wanted to kill him on the spot, but the need to protect Cerros overtook me.

"He's gone," Poppy called. When I turned to face her, she

continued, "He ran out the door. My father saw him."

Lucien ran into the hall. My eyes met Flinn's, and anger rushed through me. He had taken Poppy; he had taken her memories.

My anger turned back to Enley. How had he escaped? When I left him, he had been unconscious. The timing burned at me. If Cerros hadn't needed my help, I would have had the chance to kill Enley once and for all.

The fire in my chest intensified. I fell to my knees. As the new mark burned me from the inside out, a guttural scream escaped me. The smell of burning flesh overtook the coppery scent of blood. My fingers clenched the ground. I dug my fingernails into the packed, dry dirt. My chest tightened and my breath hitched. Slim fingers curled around mine and the pain finally subsided.

When I looked up, Poppy was before me. I exhaled slowly, letting the relief wash over me, releasing the tension in my muscles. Her skin was warm, and her touch calmed me. My hands trembled, and I clung to her. Now that the mark had settled, the pain moved to my shoulder. Blood covered my arm, and I knew the wounds needed to be bandaged.

Lucien ran into the room, out of breath. "He's gone. I'm going to check upstairs, but my guess is he ran."

I tensed. Enley wouldn't get away with this. I was going to kill him. Poppy squeezed my hands, bringing me back. Her eyes darted to my shoulder, taking in the wound. She reached into her pocket, removing a white cloth. She carefully wiped the blood.

"I knew this would be useful," she said, her lips pulled into a smile.

When I saw the napkin the magmar had given her, I shook my head. I relaxed into her touch. We would finally get our chance at happiness.

Poppy was finally mine and I would follow her anywhere.

POPPY

THREE MONTHS LATER

I looked out the window, watching Thaniel train with Lucien in the courtyard. They had been practicing for a few hours and I was getting restless. I could only watch them in short bursts before the anxiety crept in. Every thrust of the sword brought me back to Greymoore Manor. Even though Enley hadn't been found, I believed he had given up his one-sided feud.

After a quick stop at the inn, Thaniel brought me, Addie, and my parents to White Bridge. I didn't remember the first few days back. It felt like a dream. As much as I protested, he wanted to give me a few days alone with my parents. While I appreciated the sentiment, I missed him too much.

For their part, my parents were apologetic. They had acted out of fear—fear of the unknown, fear of the Ashton-Dumont curse, and fear of losing me. But no matter how many times they apologized, a part of me couldn't forgive them for taking my memories and replacing them with lies. I had learned my mother traded the last possession of my grandmother's—a gold ring—for the memory powder. In time, I would probably forgive them, but now, my heart was broken. Even though leaving my parents and Addie was hard, leaving for Marwood with Thaniel had been the right decision.

"Are you even listening?" Thea's voice interrupted my thoughts.

I turned from the window. Halo looked up at me, his tail wagging as I readjusted myself on the chair. He licked my leg before sitting at my feet. I couldn't leave him at the inn. I was meant to find the dog. Even if Thaniel didn't like to admit it, he was growing on him. Just as Scraps had. He had even named him.

"Yes," I lied.

She had most likely been talking about her upcoming trip to Lockporte. She was going with the king and queen to extend an olive branch to the royal family. There was more to the visit, but I was still learning. Thankfully, Thaniel and I had been excused. Cerros would stay in Marwood as well.

"So, red or blue?"

I turned away. "Blue, of course."

Thea sighed. "You weren't listening. I asked what my brother gave you for your birthday. The red or blue was only a test to see if you were listening."

I looked out the window again, surprised to see the court-yard empty. That meant he would be on his way up.

"Nothing," I answered. At Thea's concerned look, I added, "I told him I didn't want anything."

The past three months had gone by so fast, I had almost forgotten my birthday. Time seemed to pass differently in Marwood. There wasn't the same rush, or hustle, found in White Bridge.

"Don't worry, I'll talk to him. The way he carried on when you disappeared—"

"Let's not bring that up," Thaniel said. "I'm finally happy."

My stomach fluttered at his voice. "Me too."

Thaniel offered me his hand. "I want to take you somewhere, before everyone gets here."

I couldn't stop the smile. Thaniel brought something out in me unlike anything I had ever experienced.

"Have fun," Thea said. "I'll greet your parents; they should be here soon."

I took Thaniel's hand. "Thank you."

My parents and Addie were coming to Marwood for the weekend to celebrate my birthday. I was excited to see them.

Thaniel led me outside, past the cottage to the gate. I narrowed my eyes. I could guess where he was taking me. Since learning the truth about the poppy field, we hadn't been back. I missed it. I still had dreams about it, laying in the sea of flowers, the sun warming my face, but it wasn't the same since learning each poppy represented a life lost.

When we reached the field, Thaniel stopped walking. He dropped my hand and reached into his jacket pocket. He withdrew a small rectangle box.

"It's been a while since we've been here," he said. "But it still holds a special place in my heart." He paused.

I smiled up at him. I didn't think I could say anything without crying.

"I love you, Poppy," he added, handing me the box. "Happy birthday."

I took the box, trailing my finger over the lid. I wasn't ready for a ring. While we had talked about marriage, I still needed time.

Our eyes met.

"This isn't…"

He laughed. "No. I know you're not ready."

I let out the breath I had been holding. I placed my finger on the lid, lifting it open. A warmth spread through me when I saw the caramels.

"I don't think you got to enjoy them on your sixteenth birthday."

My chest tightened. There were still so many missing memories. Since returning to Marwood, no others had returned. I was beginning to worry that they would never come, that they were lost forever.

Thaniel placed his finger under my chin, lifting my head until our eyes met. "What's wrong?"

I covered the caramels. "I'm worried the rest of my memories won't return. There's so much I'm missing."

He smiled. "We can create new ones."

I nodded. He was right. Those memories may never return, but I would make new ones. I wrapped my arms around his neck, pulling him close. His lips met mine, sending sharp tingles down my spine.

I had a lifetime of new memories to look forward to.

ABOUT THE AUTHOR

Jessica LeMore is the author of the fantasy romance series The Shadow Marked, as well as the YA fantasy series The Mirrored Crown. She lives in upstate New York. You can visit her online at www.jessicarlemore.com.

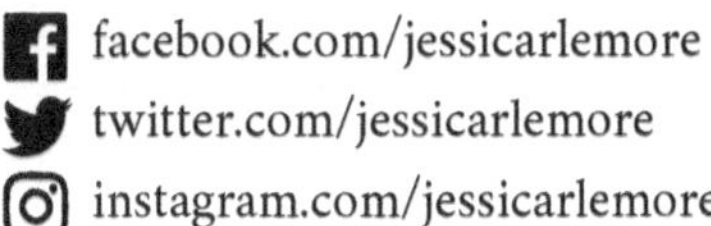